Dear Diary,

The mystery is no clos[...]
becoming more compli[...]
why has no one come fo[...]
baby girl?

The entire hospital staff has become like one big family,
fretting over our little orphan. Or maybe she's not an
orphan. The blood tests Annabelle Peters ran revealed that
the man and woman killed in the car crash weren't this
baby's parents. So who is?

Baby Chris. That's what Shana has named her. I'm
convinced the baby's relatives will be found, wherever they
are. It took a lot of searching and a lot of luck, but I
finally found my father and at the same time discovered
my stepsister, Shana. What a joy she's been to work with at
the hospital's new child-care center. Shana's a dream with
children, and she's the perfect person to be looking after our
mystery baby.

The fact that she's sharing the responsibility with
Keith Hewitt has me a little stunned, I have to admit.
Whenever Shana gets anywhere near the director of
social services, the atmosphere feels as tension-filled as
the air before a summer storm. You just know an eruption
is soon to follow.

Shana and Keith playing mommy and daddy up at
Keith's cabin all week? Well, spontaneous combustion is
guaranteed. I just hope the flames they spark are the sexy,
passionate kind.

Till tomorrow,

Alexandra

DEBRA WEBB

was born in Scottsboro, Alabama, to parents who
taught her that anything is possible if you want
it badly enough. She began writing at age nine.
Eventually she met and married the man of her
dreams, and tried some other occupations, including
selling vacuum cleaners and working in a factory, a
day-care center, a hospital and a department store.
When her husband joined the military, they moved
to Berlin, Germany, and Debra became a secretary in
the commanding general's office. By 1985 they were
back in the States, and finally moved to Tennessee, to
a small town where everyone knows everyone else.
With the support of her husband and two beautiful
daughters, Debra took up writing again, looking to
mystery and movies for inspiration. In 1998 her
dream of writing for Harlequin came true. You can
write to Debra with your comments at P.O. Box 64,
Huntland, Tennessee 37345, or visit her Web site at
www.debrawebb.com to find out exciting news about
her next book.

Forrester Square

LEGACIES . LIES . LOVE .

DEBRA WEBB

NOBODY'S BABY

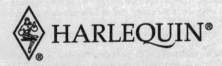

HARLEQUIN®

TORONTO • NEW YORK • LONDON
AMSTERDAM • PARIS • SYDNEY • HAMBURG
STOCKHOLM • ATHENS • TOKYO • MILAN • MADRID
PRAGUE • WARSAW • BUDAPEST • AUCKLAND

HARLEQUIN BOOKS
225 Duncan Mill Road, Don Mills,
Ontario, Canada M3B 3K9

ISBN 0-373-61281-8

NOBODY'S BABY

Debra Webb is acknowledged as the author of this work.

Dear Reader,

Welcome to the world of Forrester Square! You'll find lots of love, hope and mystery in these wonderful stories. Family is so important, and the families of Forrester Square have roots that run deep in Seattle's rich soil. But the secrets run a little deep, as well. Though it may be true that everyone has at least one secret, there are those who have more than you could possibly imagine.

I hope you'll enjoy Shana and Keith's story as they learn to trust...and to fall in love. But they're not in this alone—there's the mystery baby. The last thing confirmed bachelor Keith Hewitt expected to do was spend his holiday weekend with a ready-made family. Follow this poignant journey as both Keith and Shana fall in love not only with each other but with the baby whose name they don't even know.

Happy reading!

Debra Webb

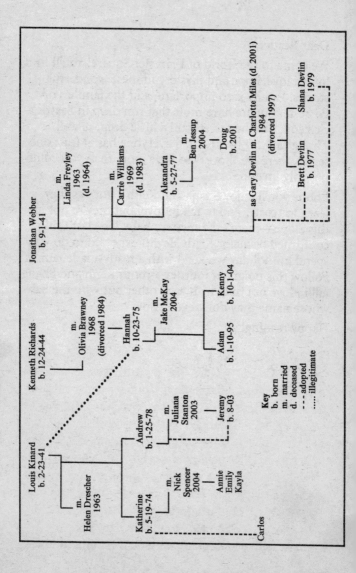

Key
b. born
m. married
d. deceased
- - - adopted
..... illegitimate

Louis Kinard
b. 2-23-41

m.
Helen Drescher
1963

Katherine
b. 5-19-74

m.
Nick Spencer
2004

Annie   Emily   Kayla

Andrew
b. 1-25-78

m.
Juliana Stanton
2003

Jeremy
b. 8-03

Carlos

Kenneth Richards
b. 12-24-44

m.
Olivia Brawney
1968
(divorced 1984)

Hannah
b. 10-23-75

m.
Jake McKay
2004

Adam
b. 1-10-95

Kenny
b. 10-1-04

Jonathan Webber
b. 9-1-41

m.
Linda Freyley
1963
(d. 1964)

m.
Carrie Williams
1969
(d. 1983)

Alexandra
b. 5-27-77

m.
Ben Jessup
2004

Doug
b. 2001

as Gary Devlin m. Charlotte Miles (d. 2001)
1984
(divorced 1997)

Brett Devlin
b. 1977

Shana Devlin
b. 1979

CHAPTER ONE

KEITH HEWITT STOOD in the corridor outside the operating rooms of Seattle Memorial Hospital and took in his friend's haggard demeanor. Detective Jaron Dorsey had seen too much today...gotten too close. An all-too-familiar hurt and weariness—an expression Keith had seen two years ago when Jaron had lost his wife—was written across his face. This kind of tragedy affected everyone who became a part of it, from the cops to the hospital staff. Like a row of dominoes, once the first piece fell, there was no stopping the chain reaction.

The accident had been a bad one, involving a car and an eighteen-wheeler. The truck driver had walked away unscathed, but the family in the car...well, that was a different story. The father was DOA. The child was seemingly unharmed. But the mother...

"You don't want to watch this," Keith said firmly to his friend. The man didn't *need* to watch this—he was clearly too close already. The horror had transported him back two years to his own tragic loss.

"The hell I don't." Jaron shook his head. "I'm with this one to the end. How's the baby?"

"Ben Jessup's checking her out," Keith told him,

knowing any further argument about watching the surgery would be pointless. "The preliminary word is good. Unless, of course, he finds something in the X rays or scans. But he doesn't expect to. The girl's got a strong pair of lungs," he added with a weary chuckle. "It seems the young lady's hungry and she's let the entire hospital know it."

"Great." Jaron smiled, but his heart wasn't in it.

Keith eyed his friend closely once more. "I hear you played the hero to the hilt."

"I didn't have much choice."

"Don't tell me," Keith said wryly, "you were just doing your job." He put a hand on his friend's shoulder, noting again the look of strain on his face and the bandages on his hands. "You should go home, Jaron. Tuck in your kids and crawl into bed yourself. You don't need to watch this." Keith winced inwardly as he considered what the bandages likely covered. The car had gone up in flames. "You in much pain?"

"Only when I laugh, and I'm not laughing."

"I can see that." Keith openly conceded defeat. "Come on. Let's see how this is going to play out. It sounds pretty grim." He said the last with as much hope as he could muster, but he knew it wasn't going to be good. Not good at all.

Once their street clothes and shoes were appropriately covered, Keith led Jaron through the sterile territory beyond the beige doors and on to the viewing area for the operating rooms. "She's in four," Keith said as he ushered his friend toward the window at the end of the corridor. "We can watch from there."

"Not much hope for her, huh?"

Keith shook his head. "Unfortunately not."

"So, what are you doing here?" Jaron asked as his gaze settled on the figures working frantically on the other side of the glass.

"I'm here for the family." Keith shrugged. "There's not a lot I can do as social services director of the hospital, but someone who cares about this woman will eventually land in my office—someone who'll wish they could have been here. For their sake, I'm here." He turned his attention to the trauma team and then he prayed. He'd been called down here from the sanctuary of his office because a child was involved. A child who would most likely be orphaned before this night was through.

"If you want someone who was with the mother all the way, it'll be Dr. Annabelle Peters they should speak to," Jaron said, his voice harsh in a way that had nothing to do with exhaustion and everything to do with resentment.

A frown furrowed Keith's brow. What was this about? "You don't like our Dr. Peters?"

"She's a bit…cold."

Annabelle could give that impression. "She keeps to herself," Keith admitted as he switched on the monitor so they could hear as well as see the drama on the other side of the glass.

"There's too much bleeding." A voice came over the speaker. "I'm having trouble locating—"

"Clamp—now!" another voice shouted, drowning out the first.

"Blood pressure's dropping."

Keith turned off the monitor as quickly as he'd turned it on. "Maybe we'll just watch," he said grimly.

The silence thickened for a moment as the scene played out beneath the blinding overhead lights. Nurses and doctors performed like a well-choreographed team of dancers. Each move, each uttered word was met with a corresponding reaction or response. No one faltered or missed a step.

Minutes ticked by…precious minutes marked by a downward spiral in the patient's condition.

His voice hollow in the cold hush of the corridor, Jaron asked, "How long has Dr. Peters been at Seattle Memorial?"

Keith was glad for the question—anything to divert his attention for just one moment. "She came from New Jersey a while back, and the hospital was pleased to get her. She's the best E.R. director we've had."

"She seems a cold fish…in my opinion."

Keith thought about that for a moment. "She's efficient. Gets the job done and doesn't cut corners."

Jaron arched a skeptical eyebrow. "You don't like her, either?"

"I didn't say that," Keith snapped before he caught himself, irritated that his own misgivings about the newest doctor on staff had shown through. "She just keeps to herself, that's all." He shrugged, trying to decide how to say what he felt without having it come out the wrong way again. "She hasn't mixed with the rest of the staff in the usual way. She lives in one of the hospital apartments, so there's some interaction off duty with the other in-house residents, but not to the usual extent." He spread his hands, palms up. "Maybe she simply prefers her own company."

Jaron looked at the woman in question now. "She's not coming across as a warm and caring human being, if you ask me."

The comment surprised Keith. Jaron wasn't usually so judgmental. "Why do you say that?"

"She's been less than helpful in this investigation. She won't push…"

"She won't push what?"

"I need to know who this Jane Doe is," Jaron said tightly. "There's a kid involved, and the car they were driving was stolen. It could take weeks to ferret out a name."

"Surely someone will be looking for them," Keith suggested. "A family with a young child just doesn't disappear without people asking after them. The stolen car could—"

"But if she already knows…" Jaron interrupted.

"Annabelle?" Keith couldn't believe that. "What are you saying? Are you telling me she knows the woman's identity and isn't telling? That's absurd." The doctor might be a little standoffish, he'd give Jaron that, but she was a professional to the bone.

Jaron never took his eyes off Annabelle, his scrutiny intensifying with each passing moment. "She knows something."

"Then she'll tell us." Keith turned his attention back to the desperate scene on the other side of the glass.

"All I'm saying is that she should have pushed for the information," Jaron challenged. "She should have delayed this surgery until we had a name."

His words stunned Keith. "And let her patient die? I'm certain you don't mean that, Jaron."

"But…"

Realization dawned on Keith. "I see the problem. You're kicking yourself because you didn't push more for an identity at the scene."

The truth in that statement hardened Jaron's already strained features. "I had the chance in the ambulance on the way here," he said bitterly. "I could have pressed…."

"But you didn't," Keith guessed, "because it seemed unimportant in the face of the woman's fight for life. Funny thing is, I'm certain that's exactly the way Annabelle sees it."

A muscle ticked in the detective's jaw. "She needs to see the big picture. The woman's dying…. The kid—"

"This isn't two years ago," Keith said quietly, seeing the big picture quite clearly himself. He and Jaron had become friends based on that terrible tragedy. "That isn't your wife on that table, and the baby isn't your child." The tragic death of Jaron's wife had left a single father with two small children to raise. No wonder he was having trouble keeping his objectivity in this case.

Jaron sighed heavily and pressed his forehead against the glass.

"Go home," Keith suggested. "Let us do what has to be done."

"Nope. You're here because you care, and so am I."

"Jaron—"

"Leave it. Let's just wait."

Keith had a very bad feeling that their wait was almost over as his gaze came to rest on the patient whose life hung in the balance. Jaron wasn't the only one fighting demons from the past. Keith swallowed, the muscles of his throat struggling with the effort. But talking about Jaron's tragedy had kept his own at bay.

A distant buzzing started in Keith's ears. He would need to contact next of kin, he told himself in an effort to stay on track. Someone would have to take care of the child until... And just like that, Keith was eight years old again and watching his own mother die in an E.R. not unlike this one. He felt oddly numb, disassociated from the events currently happening around him. This wasn't the first time he'd seen a patient die...but somehow it was different. This situation hit far too close to home. Memories he'd just as soon forget loomed in the corners of his mind. He forced them back. He would not relive the past.

Jaron was already doing enough of that for both of them.

SHE WAS FINALLY ASLEEP.

A sigh of relief seeped past Shana Devlin's lips as she eased quietly from the room. Colorful artwork and event announcements lined the wide gallery hallway that separated the various rooms of Round the Clock child-care center and opened into the well-appointed lobby and reception area, with its wide glass doors. She glanced at the wall clock—7:30 p.m. Little Kayley Garner was finally asleep. Shana smiled. Kayley had fought until the bitter end, but the four-year-old had ultimately lost the battle with the sandman.

Luckily for Shana, her other charges had gone right to sleep practically the moment their heads hit the pillow. The daughter of one of the doctors on staff at Seattle Memorial, Kayley was every bit as stubborn as her handsome daddy. But Shana loved the child immensely, and saw a little of herself in those mischievous blue eyes. She peeked in on Detective Jaron Dorsey's two children, who'd finally given in to the sandman themselves. Ricky and Tina were beautiful children and had adapted well to their father's occasional late pickups. After all, a detective never knew when a case was going to keep him on duty beyond the expected hour. Round the Clock was the perfect child-care setup for cops and doctors, since the center was open twenty-four hours a day.

As soon as Shana had gotten the call that Jaron would be late, she'd settled the kids in for an extended stay. Now she could relax a bit. Making a quick detour into the kitchen, she poured herself a cup of coffee. She added two packages of sugar and stirred thoughtfully. Working the evening shift had its advantages. Sure, the hours between four and eight were tough, even with only five children to oversee. And especially on a Friday evening. The kids were really wound up. But once they were tucked in, the final couple of hours gave Shana time to relax and unwind herself. By eleven, the end of her shift, she was ready to go home and fall into her own bed. Thankfully, she didn't have far to go, since she had taken an apartment in the hospital.

Although the apartments were traditionally reserved for doctors and nurses, few took advantage of the benefit. Most of the doctors lived in expensive homes in Seattle's ritzy neighborhoods. And most of the nurses had husbands and homes of their own. A few of the younger, single staff members opted for the apartments, but that left several open, and Shana had one of them. No late-night drives home for her.

That drive was one of the reasons no one else liked this shift at the center. Shana could understand. Not to mention that those who had husbands and children wanted to be at home with them in the evening. Shana had neither.

That thought nagged at her. But she was only twenty-five, she argued. A husband and kids would come eventually. It was far too early for her to start feeling sorry for herself, that was for sure. And it wasn't as if she didn't get her share of invitations to dinner and such. As new as she was to Seattle, she'd already settled in nicely. She simply hadn't met anyone who interested her yet, at least not enough to make her want to pursue an actual relationship. There was plenty of time. She smiled. And plenty of eligible men. She refused to consider that there might be another reason she was still single…a little something called trust.

Retreating to the reception area, Shana checked the volume and the channel setting on the monitor before she sat down. All was as it should be. The screen was split into four sections, each currently displaying an area where children slept. A simple change in channel would reveal four other rooms of the center. The location of the various monitors allowed for constant surveillance of the children, even when she wasn't in the same room with them. Now she'd have a chance to take that much-needed break.

She relaxed into an upholstered chair and sipped her coffee, moaning appreciatively as the warm rich liquid tantalized her taste buds, soothed her throat. She'd made it half decaf and half regular, so she could get a little jolt of caffeine without worrying that it would prevent sleep later.

Keeping a close watch on the children via the monitor in the corner above the receptionist's desk, Shana considered her new life in Seattle.

To say that it was different from her old one back home in Nebraska was a vast understatement. She smiled as she thought of her recently discovered stepsister, Alexandra Webber. Alex, as Shana preferred to call her, had tracked down her father's adopted children, Shana and Brett, with the intention of uniting her remaining family. Shana's own mother had died a few years back, leaving her and her brother all alone in the world. Their biological father was dead now, too. Their mother had divorced him when Shana and Brett were kids, but Gary Devlin had made an excellent stepfather, at least until his illness.

Shana couldn't help but resent that her mother had given their stepfather the heave-ho at the first signs of Alzheimer's. Unfortunately, Shana and her brother hadn't known the whole situation—and never would have known what became of the man who'd raised and loved them as his own, had it not been for Alexandra.

Gary Devlin, they'd learned recently, was not their stepfather's real name. He was Jonathan Webber, formerly of Seattle. Although now it was safe for him to be in Seattle, Jonathan had had to enter the Witness Protection Program twenty years ago and take on a new identity. In Nebraska he'd met and married Charlotte Miles, and had, in time, adopted Shana and Brett.

Learning of her stepfather's whereabouts and that she had a stepsister in Seattle, Shana had gladly accepted Alexandra's invitation to join them. Shana was ready for something different, ready to move on. Brett didn't share her enthusiasm. He'd resented their own father's failure to stand up to their overbearing mother, and he'd resented their mother even more. Then, of course, when their stepfather left as well, that was just one more thing for Brett to hold against their mother and make him question the sanctity of marriage. He swore the last thing he wanted was more family. That trust thing again.

Shana sighed and set her coffee aside. Her new life would be truly complete if only she could persuade Brett to join her in Seattle, even for a visit. If nothing else, he should come and see their stepfather while Gary—Jonathan—still had the rare lucid day.

The sound of the main entry door being unlocked and then opened drew Shana's attention in that direction. She smiled when her gaze fell upon Alexandra. The door whooshed closed behind her, and without pause, she locked it.

"Speak of the devil," Shana teased, pushing to her feet to accept her sister's hug.

Alexandra drew back from the embrace. "And just what is that supposed to mean?" She smiled in turn, affection shining in her eyes.

"I was just thinking about you." Shana frowned. "What are you doing here so late? You're supposed to be at home with Ben, planning your wedding. I know it's not till June, but it will be here before you know it."

Alexandra rolled her eyes and made a disparaging sound. "Believe me, I know. Who would have thought that getting married could be so complicated?" Another smile inched across her face. "Not that I'm complaining, mind you."

"I wouldn't be complaining, either. Ben's a real catch. But you haven't answered my question. What *are* you doing here?"

"I left those bridal magazines that Hannah insisted

I look through in my office." Hannah was Alexandra's good friend and one of the founders of Forrester Square Day Care. Although Ben now owned both the day care and Round the Clock, Hannah had agreed to stay on at Forrester Square to help out her friend. Alexander threw up her hands. "Don't say it, I know. How could a prospective bride forget her bridal magazines?" She shrugged. "Too many irons in the fire, I think."

"You've got that right," Shana scolded gently. "With Hannah on maternity leave, you've got your hands full." Shana couldn't help but worry about the sister she'd only just discovered. She sure didn't want her working herself into the ground. Nor could she blame Hannah for taking time off to be with her new baby boy. Hannah had named him Kenny, after her father, Kenneth.

"I can't complain, though," Alexandra protested readily. "Carmen has really helped out by taking over the day-to-day operations at Forrester Square Day Care." Her eyes twinkled. Though they weren't the same color as her father's, there was something about the twinkle, the exuberance in her face, that reminded Shana of him. "You'll never guess what I discovered today," Alexandra said in a hushed, conspiratorial tone.

Shana knew it had to be good from the look on Alexandra's face. "Don't keep me in suspense, Alex—tell me!"

"Carmen and Russ..." Alexandra hesitated. "You've met Russ Tidwell, haven't you? He's Amy's father—the teenage aide at Forrester Square Day Care. Hannah kept Amy and Will's baby for them while they were pulling things together.''

Shana nodded. ''Yes. I met them at the day care, and you told me all about them.'' Russ had been totally opposed to Amy keeping her baby, and had made life miserable for his teenage daughter and her boyfriend. But the stroke Russ suffered seemed to have changed the man's temperament, and he had reconciled with Amy and Will, who was now her husband.

''Well.'' Alexandra looked covertly from side to side. ''Russ asked Carmen out to dinner.''

Carmen was the head teacher at Forrester Square. A widow and grandmother, she had taken Amy under her wing and given Russ a piece of her mind on more than one occasion. Shana's eyes widened in disbelief. ''No!''

Alexandra nodded.

''That's great.'' Alexandra had told Shana that since he'd recovered from his stroke, Russ had poured his energy into making Amy, Will and his new granddaughter, Leanne, happy. He was even paying for Will's education. Shana was glad he hadn't overlooked his own needs in the process.

She resisted the urge to sigh. If only straightening out her own love life, or lack thereof, were so easy. But she forced the thoughts away. ''Did you see Hannah and the baby today?''

''Sure did. She looks so happy. I'm almost jealous.''

Shana scoffed. "Are you kidding? You've got Ben and that cute son of his."

Alexandra looked properly chagrined. "I certainly do. But I can't help wanting a baby, too. They're just so precious."

Shana suffered a little tug of want herself. Truth be told, she'd like nothing better than a husband and a baby. But good husband material wasn't easily found these days. The image of one particular man bloomed in her thoughts, but she instantly banished it. This guy was definitely not husband material. As far as Shana was concerned, he wasn't even boyfriend material. Men that good-looking couldn't be trusted. Her mother, God rest her soul, had drilled that bit of wisdom into Shana's head her entire life. And Shana's relatively few experiences with extraordinarily handsome men had lent credence to her mother's warnings.

Alexandra draped one arm around Shana's shoulders, dragging her attention back to the here and now. "Let's go find those magazines."

"I dropped by the nursing home to see Dad today," Shana told her as they moved toward Round the Clock's office. "He even recognized me."

Alexandra squeezed her shoulders. "That's great." She sighed contentedly. "I'm so glad you're here. I just wish…"

Her words trailed off wistfully, but she didn't have to say the rest. Shana knew what she meant. She wished Brett would come around, too. "I'll keep working on him," Shana promised.

After Alexandra located her bridal magazines, Shana walked her back to the door. "Have a nice weekend."

"I will." Alexandra gave her shoulder one last squeeze. "You, too."

Shana watched her go, then locked the glass doors behind her. They were kept secured after the receptionist left for the day at 6:00 p.m. Alexandra had used her key, but anyone else who wanted in had to press the buzzer and show proper I.D. Even in a hospital, a place normally considered safe, security measures had to be followed.

As Shana drifted back toward where the children were sleeping, she considered her brother. He'd always been a lone wolf, even as a kid. But there had to be a way to get him to Seattle. Once he met Alexandra and Shana's other new friends, she was sure he'd feel at home here. It wasn't as if there was anything left in the way of family back in Nebraska. Even if there had been, Brett stayed too busy with his private investigations business to notice. He'd rather stick his head in the sand and ignore everyone else. But that wouldn't stop Shana from chiseling away at that armor he stubbornly wore.

She checked on the sleeping children before returning to her now-cold coffee. *Oh well,* she thought. She preferred a quick visit from Alexandra over coffee any day. Shana took her cup to the kitchen sink and then surveyed the room at large. She'd already put away the remains of the children's evening snack, so there really wasn't anything to be done. She'd tidied the living room, turned off the television and shut down the computers in the quiet room, where the older children often did homework. Monitoring the sleeping angels was her only concern now. Absently, she rinsed her cup and wished she'd brought a good book with her tonight as she usually did.

The sudden hum of the buzzer startled Shana. She pressed a hand to her throat and took a calming breath. She seldom had company after eight. Most of the parents were employed at Seattle Memorial and didn't pick up their kids until a few minutes after her shift ended, since theirs ended at eleven, as well. Maybe it was Jaron Dorsey. But she'd gotten the impression that his business was going to take some time. She hoped there wasn't a problem.

The buzzer sounded again. Thankfully it was not connected to the sleeping room. All she needed right now was five whining kids wanting to know what was going on and when their mommy or daddy would come.

The annoying drone resonated yet again before she could dry her hands. Someone was clearly impatient. Hastening her step, she hurried from the kitchen, hoping against hope there wasn't an emergency with one of the parents. They all felt like friends now. Good friends. Something that had been missing in her life for entirely too long.

Shana burst into the reception area and stopped dead in her tracks when she identified the man waiting on the other side of the glass double doors.

Keith Hewitt.

What was *he* doing here at this time of night?

And then she looked at that face, and all rational thought deserted her like rats leaving a sinking ship.

Keith Hewitt was over six feet tall, and had broad shoulders and the best butt she'd ever seen on a man. Despite that amazing body, it was his face that took every woman's breath. His features were lean and chiseled, framed by thick, wavy chestnut hair, and his eyes were the color of liquid gold. But it was his mouth that did the most damage to her nervous system. That mouth was wide, full, masterfully sculpted—far too perfect to belong on a masculine face, no matter how incredibly handsome.

The sad part was, he knew all of the above. Keith Hewitt, aka Seattle Memorial's heartthrob and most eligible bachelor, was well aware of just how good-looking he was, and he used that knowledge to his advantage at every opportunity. He was arrogant, defiant and…and Shana hated him. With every fiber of her being.

She winced inwardly. Okay, maybe she didn't hate him. But she disliked him immensely. He personified everything her mother had warned her about. And as much as she disliked him, she had the distinct impression that the feeling was mutual. Foolishly, that idea stung her ego. Apparently Keith had asked out every other single female on staff. What was wrong with *her*?

Her gaze narrowed suspiciously as he pressed the buzzer yet again and glared at her as if she'd lost her ever-loving mind. Just what did he want? This was her territory. He had his own office on…

Only then did Shana notice the squirming infant in his arms.

"Oh God," she breathed as she raced to the door and flipped the lock. She jerked the door open wide. "I'm sorry—"

"Ms. Devlin," he snapped above the child's incessant wailing, "I know you were hired because you're the boss's sister, but you could at least try to behave in a professional manner."

Fury whipped through Shana, stiffening her spine. "I beg your pardon?"

"You stood there—" he nodded to the middle of the room "—staring at me as if I'd grown a second head and sprouted a tail. Couldn't you see I had a child in my possession?"

Possession was right, Shana noted with mounting annoyance. He held the baby as if it were an alien object of dubious origin.

"Let me take the baby," she said, rescuing the infant from his awkward embrace. She ignored the heat that licked a path up her arms the moment their hands touched. She hated that he could invoke a response from her so easily. Whenever they came in close contact, it happened.

Instantly forgetting the intolerable man, Shana snuggled the pink-clad infant close to her chest. "Hello, sweetie pie," she cooed, then made the silly sounds all babies responded to. The infant stilled immediately. "What's your name, precious?"

"She doesn't have a name," Keith stated matter-of-factly.

Shana shifted toward him, affecting an expression every bit as testy as his own. "She has to have a name."

He bristled. "What I mean to say," he amended pointedly, "is that we don't know her name. Her parents died in an automobile accident this evening. The car is listed as stolen, so I may have trouble tracking down the next of kin."

"Oh, how sad." Gently bouncing the baby in her arms, Shana peered down at her. "You poor baby girl."

"How did you do that?"

His bewildered tone brought her head up. "Do what?"

He seemed at a loss for words, then shrugged casually. "That thing you did that made her stop crying. She howled the whole trip from the E.R. to my office and then here." He looked at the baby, then at Shana, and shrugged again. "I was certain Dr. Jessup was wrong when he insisted the child was unharmed by the accident."

Shana resisted the urge to tell him that girls were born with "pig" radar. "Practice, *Mr. Hewitt*."

He nodded stiffly. "I see. Well, in any event, I'll let you know what I find out." He backed up a step. "You'll need to take care of the child for the next few hours until other arrangements are made."

"No problem."

He backed up another step. "Fine."

He started to turn around, but Shana stopped him. She couldn't help the grin that stretched across her lips. "Do you plan to take that with you?"

He frowned. "Excuse me?"

She gestured to his shoulder. "The diaper bag. I might need it."

Color surged from beneath the crisp white collar of his shirt. "Of course." He lifted the bag from one broad shoulder and offered it to her.

Shana took a step in his direction. She didn't want to touch him again. She extended her hand in hopes that he'd simply drop the strap onto her palm.

But he didn't.

He placed his right hand under hers and held it steady while he deposited the strap into her open palm with his left. She shivered at the feel of his long fingers as they brushed her sensitive skin. That amber gaze never left hers. She didn't miss the little flecks of gold that sparkled there. And she knew just what that meant. He enjoyed the fact that he made her uncomfortable…made her respond to his touch. That was something else he did whenever they encountered each other—teased and flirted. He seemed to enjoy making her hot and bothered, only to ask someone else to go out with him.

She jerked her hand back, the bag in tow. "Thank you."

He smiled—one of those killer smiles that was all lethal charm and drop-dead gorgeous. "Thank *you*, Ms. Devlin."

Anger making her breath ragged, she hooked the

strap onto her shoulder and shot daggers at him with her eyes. He hesitated at the door, and the smile that lingered on those sensual lips widened at her deadly glower. God, why didn't he just go?

"I'll be back."

Then he was gone.

Shana marched over to the door and locked it behind him. She refused to consider whether his parting words were a threat or just fair warning.

She smiled down at the baby. She wasn't going to waste her time thinking about some arrogant, pigheaded, male chauvinist jerk who thought he was God's gift to women.

She had better things to do.

CHAPTER TWO

"WE HAVE A PROBLEM."

Seth Nannery's groggy response came over the telephone line. "Keith? What's going on? What time is it?"

It wasn't that late. But obviously Seth had gone home after work and taken a nap. Keith had clearly awakened him from a deep sleep. "Seven fifty-five," Keith retorted, too weary himself to work up much exasperation.

"What's going on?" Seth asked again.

"There was a fatal automobile crash tonight. The driver and his wife were killed, but their infant daughter survived. I need to contact next of kin."

Keith could practically hear Seth scratching his head in confusion.

"I'm with you so far. What do you need from me?"

"Since there was no other form of ID that survived the crash, the investigating officer ran the plates." Keith forked his fingers through his hair. This was simply too surreal. "The car was stolen."

"That's bad," Seth said slowly.

"Exactly."

Silence vibrated along the phone line for three beats.

"So the dead people are John and Jane Doe, as far as the hospital is concerned," Seth offered.

"Don't forget Baby Doe." And therein lay the crux of Keith's immediate problem. "I can't contact next of kin if I don't know where to start looking."

He heard a heavy sigh. "Okay. I'm on my way in. Who's the investigating officer?"

"Detective Jaron Dorsey from Seattle PD is in the E.R. talking to Dr. Peters and her staff right now. He's a good man. If anyone can get to the bottom of this, he can. I knew if the press got wind of it, there could be repercussions, so I called you. You know how they love to play up this kind of tragedy."

"Of course. I'll be there in thirty minutes."

Seth's words lacked conviction. He was new to the hospital. Maybe the idea of his first confrontation with the press concerned him.

"I'll meet you in the E.R.," Keith said in closing.

"Keith," Seth said before ending the call, "what'll become of the baby until…" he cleared his throat "…until next of kin is located?"

"I'll contact Child Services and they'll find a temporary foster home or facility to care for her."

A new kind of tension echoed across the phone line. "See you in thirty."

Keith dropped the receiver into its cradle and considered Seth Nannery for a moment. He was single, smart. Hell, the guy could sell snow in Alaska. That's what made him such a good PR representative for the hospital. But that didn't explain away the worry—dread, even—that Keith had heard in his voice when he'd asked about the child.

Keith shrugged. He had his own problems and didn't need to waste time analyzing anyone else's. Not even his friend Jaron's. Keith thought he'd long ago gotten his own nightmare under control, but tonight in the E.R. it had come rushing back to him. Every second of every excruciating minute. He closed his eyes and braced his head in his hands. He didn't want to remember. He only wanted to do his job.

That was how he kept the haunting memories at bay. He worked hard to make sure no one ever felt the way he'd been made to feel…the way his father had been made to feel. Keith would do everything in his power, would use every asset at his disposal, to make sure no child—no parent—ever suffered under his watch.

Thirty minutes later, as promised, Seth Nannery entered the hospital through the emergency room doors. Keith waited in the receiving area. He immediately led Seth to Jaron, who looked madder than hell. Keith's gut tightened at the thought of how personally the detective was taking this. Keith was taking it just as hard, only he wasn't letting anyone see his angst.

"Can you spare a few minutes?" he asked Jaron. "This is Seth Nannery." He gestured to Seth. "He's the hospital's new public relations director, and we need to make some decisions."

"Fine," Jaron replied, though he didn't look happy.

"Seth Nannery, Detective Jaron Dorsey," Keith added.

The two men started to shake hands but made a mutual decision not to, considering Jaron's bandaged hands.

Jaron pursed his lips thoughtfully. "Planning a statement for the press would be good. It might even be helpful in discovering the identities of the parents."

Seth paled but quickly recovered. "I agree."

Keith tried not to frown. What was with Nannery? Keith had heard all about his reputation as a spin doctor. Surely the man could handle this. "Let's go to my office," Keith suggested.

Seth nodded, seemingly relieved, and the two men followed Keith to the main lobby. From there they took the elevator to the third floor. All the offices were dark except social services. Keith showed them through the anteroom and finally to his own domain.

"Have a seat." As he settled into his leather chair he gestured to the two upholstered chairs that flanked his desk.

"So what have we got?" Seth asked when he'd sat down.

Jaron did the same and then shook his head. "As you know, the driver was DOA and the woman was too far gone to say much of anything." He paused, skepticism inching into his expression. "I have my doubts where Dr. Peters is concerned, however."

"What the hell is that supposed to mean?" Seth demanded.

Keith lifted a skeptical eyebrow. *Way to go, Mr. Public Relations.* "I think what Seth is asking is what kind of doubts? If you're implying her professional skills—"

"No, no. Nothing like that." Jaron took his time, considering his next words before speaking. His posture rigid, Seth sat beside him, clearly working up a head of steam. Great, Keith thought, just what they needed—a PR guy with a short fuse.

"Dr. Peters isn't telling me everything she knows," Jaron said at last. "It's just a gut feeling I have, but I'm almost sure of it."

Annabelle Peters was serious and committed to her work, but she could be aloof, that was true. Keith hoped Jaron wasn't confusing her standoffishness with something else.

"That's ridiculous," Seth grumped.

"I feel certain if Dr. Peters had any relevant information, she would share it with us," Keith insisted, his gaze fixed firmly on the detective.

Jaron shrugged. "Maybe. I've only just begun this investigation. Time will tell if she's holding out on me."

"Why would she do—" Keith started to say, but Jaron held up a bandaged hand to waylay him.

"Maybe I'm being stupid. I'm tired and my hands hurt," he confessed. "But I can't stop a gut feeling."

Silence instilled the office with mounting tension.

"What are we going to do about the child?" Seth asked. "Obviously this won't be cleared up overnight."

"Since there's really no reason to keep her hospitalized—even if there were room in the pediatric ward—Dr. Peters and I have agreed on a temporary solution," Keith explained. "The infant will stay at Round the Clock until morning. After that, we'll be stretching the rules if next of kin isn't found." He didn't look forward to making the next call.

"We have to do this right," Seth interjected.

"By law—" Jaron began.

"We have to turn her over to Child Services." Keith stated what they both knew. "Keeping her at Round the Clock for one night isn't bending the rules, since it's part of the hospital."

Seth scrubbed a hand over his face, looking more agitated by the minute. "We're going to have the press breathing down our necks on this one. I can feel it already. An abandoned baby in a child-care center. A stolen car." He exhaled mightily. "I don't like it."

Jaron agreed. "Neither do I. But handing her over to Child Services…hell, it's Columbus Day weekend. No kid should be thrust into the arms of strangers, period, much less on a holiday. I know I'd want better than that for mine," he added, his passion on the subject quite apparent.

"It's my job to follow the guidelines," Keith said, pushing all emotion aside and focusing on the facts. "Once she's released from the doctor's care, the child must be placed with a state-approved foster parent or facility. I don't want her in an institution. I'd rather leave her right here, but I don't see that we have much choice."

Seth pushed himself to his feet. "Okay." He plowed his fingers through his hair. "I'll go work on a statement for the press. I'm sure they'll run news of the accident on the front page. If it bleeds, it leads." He shook his head as if he had no tolerance for media machinations. "If we're lucky, the news will reach someone who knows these people." He took a deep breath. "If you'll excuse me, gentlemen, I have work to do."

"Don't we all," Jaron said, then hesitated. "This case seems to be getting to everyone. I'll keep you up to speed on the investigation, but meanwhile…" He looked meaningfully at Seth, then Keith. "You guys will take care of the baby?" he asked as he stood.

Keith dipped his head in agreement. "Of course." His friend was right—this one was getting to everyone.

"As soon as I've taken care of a few calls, I've gotta pick up my kids," Jaron said. "I'll let you know if I learn anything." He hesitated before starting for the door. "If the situation changes, let me know."

When the detective had gone, Keith dropped back into his chair and stared at the telephone.

It would only take one call tomorrow morning.

His part would be finished. Once he'd turned the infant over to Child Services, he could be on his way. Keith glanced at his watch. Past eight already. He had wanted to be on the road long before now. It was a one-hour drive out to the cabin. His bags were packed and in the SUV already.

He hadn't missed a Columbus Day weekend at that cabin in over twenty years, and he wasn't going to start now. Especially not this year.

All he had to do was make that call first thing in the morning.

A few more hours wouldn't hurt.

But it might just set the stage for the mystery baby's whole life. Was there anyone out there who would take care of her? Love her the way a child deserved? Or would she end up being nobody's baby?

Keith closed his eyes. He couldn't make certain things happen. The only thing he could do was find someone—a family member, a friend or, as a last resort, a foster family. He couldn't make them love this tiny infant who'd so recently been orphaned. All he could do was make sure she had someone to look after her.

Annabelle... Jaron's conviction that she was holding back information tugged at Keith's instincts. She wouldn't do that...would she? He had to talk to her before he did anything else. Maybe if they went to see the baby together, she'd admit whatever it was Jaron thought she was holding back.

Then again, Jaron could be reading too much between the lines.

Only time would tell.

SHANA WAS IN LOVE already. After Carleen, her usual replacement for the graveyard shift had agreed to come in early—two whole hours early, thankfully— Shana had decided to bathe the baby. She definitely didn't want to leave until she knew what fate had in store for little Chris. Shana smiled down at the sleeping infant. She'd dubbed her Chrissy, calling her Chris for short. After all, it was Columbus Day weekend coming up. What better name for the mystery baby who'd landed on her doorstep, so to speak?

Tonight there would only be three children, including the baby, for the midnight shift at Round the Clock, and they were all fast asleep. Jaron Dorsey was collecting his two at that very moment, and Pete Garner would be along shortly after eleven. The Dorsey children had played twenty questions about their father's bandaged hands. Shana had already heard what had happened to Detective Dorsey from Dr. Garner, who'd called down to check on his daughter. With the baby to care for, Shana had left the good detective to finish getting his kids ready to go. The man obviously loved caring for them, to the point where he was almost obsessive about seeing after their needs personally, and Ricky and Tina definitely loved their daddy.

Carleen was busy typing her thesis for her Ph.D. in child psychology on one of the computers in the quiet room. She'd offered to take over care of the infant the moment she'd arrived and heard the tragic story, but Shana had insisted on doing it herself. She'd gotten attached really quickly.

She pressed a soft kiss to the tiny girl's delicate head. The baby smelled so sweet Shana had to fight the urge to squeeze her tight against her chest.

The diaper bag had contained a couple of changes

of clothes, diapers and two cans of formula, the ready-to-use kind. Shana had opened one and warmed it in a bottle, then fed the baby. More formula would be needed soon. She sighed and pushed the rocker back into motion with one foot. That wasn't her concern, Shana thought, her heart sinking. Child Services would come and take the baby away tomorrow. She blinked back the tears that foolishly surfaced. Getting so sentimental over someone else's baby was pointless. The authorities would do what was best for little Chris. Seattle Child Services went above and beyond the call of duty, no question. But the infant's life would never be the same.

Shana forced her attention from the sleeping baby to the room at large. She had to focus on something else or cry outright. Round the Clock had three activity rooms besides this nursery, and each converted to a sleeping room after 6:00 p.m. The rooms weren't large, but they were colorfully decorated and child friendly. Shana really loved it here.

Keith Hewitt's smart-aleck remark about how she'd gotten the position more than rankled, it infuriated her. Sure, maybe she had been hired because the "boss" was her sister—or stepsister, to be exact. But Shana worked hard and did the best job she was capable of. She prided herself in that work and loved the children dearly. Though she'd started out studying nursing, she'd changed her major to early childhood development. She was well-trained. How dare the man infer otherwise? He loved to make her furious. The whole hospital was still talking about their last confrontation. They never seemed to agree on anything. And somehow they were never able to keep their disagreements low-key. Whenever they squared off, the whole world heard about it.

The shrill hum of the buzzer jerked her from the Keith Hewitt bashing session she'd been mentally poised to launch.

"Speak of the devil," she muttered, this time meaning it in the truest sense. She didn't have to get up and peek into the reception area for verification. She knew it was him.

He was back, as promised.

Shana peered down at the precious bundle, and her chest constricted. The poor baby had already lost her mother and her father, and now she was going to be plunged into a world of strangers. Shana refused to consider herself a stranger. It was different with Baby Chris and her. They'd connected. She smiled, remembering how the baby had loved her bath. Shana would swear little Chris had smiled up at her...and not one of those expressions everyone blamed on gas, either. A true, honest-to-God, toothless smile.

"She's in the nursery, Mr. Hewitt," Shana heard Carleen say, entering the gallery hall to show the way. The echoing footsteps had to belong to *him*.

"Thank you," Keith said when they paused at the door. Carleen stared wistfully up at him before floating away as if on cloud nine.

Sheesh. Did every living female on the planet have to react that way to the man? It was humiliating to the entire gender.

"We still don't have any information on the child's next of kin," he said without preamble. "She can stay here the night, but first thing in the morning I'll be forced to call in Child Services."

Shana refused to look him directly in the eye. She didn't want to get sidetracked by that handsome face or that carnal mouth. Nope, she'd just ignore all those outer trappings and do what had to be done—either argue the point or put her own spin on it.

She stood and lifted her chin firmly. "Fine. I'm supposed to be leaving soon, but I'll stay with her until she's turned over to Child Services. She doesn't need to get used to another stranger. I've bathed and fed her." She gestured to the diaper bag on the changing table. "I'll put her down for the night."

Without comment, Keith moved to the changing table and picked up the diaper bag to look through it. As if she hadn't already done that herself—and likely Detective Dorsey, as well. Shana didn't glance away quickly as she'd intended. Her gaze fixated on the way the pastel pinks, blues and yellows of the bag contrasted with the navy designer suit, the red power tie and the unwrinkled—despite the long day he'd obviously put in—white shirt. And still the man looked sexy.

Shana couldn't help herself; she had to laugh. Quietly at first, then with unrestrained mirth. *Must be hysteria,* she told herself.

That golden gaze narrowed on her. "You find something amusing, Ms. Devlin?"

It was at precisely that moment when Shana knew

she was in trouble. This man was dangerous to her ability to reason, which was exactly why she used every opportunity to argue with him. Anything else was far too dicey. Her laughter died an immediate death. She cleared her throat and lifted her chin defiantly.

"I'm sorry, Mr. Hewitt, it's just that you look so totally out of character with that bag in hand." Laughter bubbled into her throat once more, but she swallowed it back. He was right. There was nothing funny about any of this.

"And why is that?" he asked, as if her foolish behavior had some deeper meaning that he intended to uncover.

She shrugged. "I don't know. Maybe because you don't look like the fatherly type."

Oops. She'd hit a nerve. Those intense eyes literally crackled with ire.

"What type do I look like?" he demanded, his tone low and lethal. She shivered at the sound, then silently railed at herself for doing so. He took a step in her direction. She shivered again and cuddled the baby closer.

Shaking her head as much at her own foolish behavior as at his, she hastened to assure him, "I didn't mean to insult you. It's just that…" She cleared her throat again, suddenly grappling for a response. How the heck had she let this get started? "Well, you know the female staff has voted you 'most eligible bachelor' for three years running now." She was sunk. How did she explain without being openly negative about him personally? "I mean…well, fatherhood and *that* just don't go together, to my way of thinking."

"I see."

He was ticked off now. A muscle had started to twitch in that handsome jaw. Oh well, it served him right. He'd earned the reputation, so might as well abide the consequences. After all, he was only too happy to get personal with her. His remark about how she'd gotten her job came immediately to mind. She squared her shoulders and shot a quelling look back at him. "Do you?" she asked, just to be ornery.

The stare-down lasted ten full seconds.

He looked away first. "As I said, I'll put in the call first thing in the morning, and someone will pick up the child."

Shana's bravado wilted. "Will a family take care of her until next of kin can be located?" *Please let them be extra kind, caring people,* she silently beseeched.

He blinked. "The likelihood of finding someone on a holiday weekend isn't good. Next week perhaps, if no next of kin is located."

Anxiety surged inside her. "Where will she go?"

He kept his gaze focused on the infant in her arms. "There's a facility—"

"A facility?" she demanded incredulously. "You intend to turn this baby over to an unfeeling, clinical facility?" The infant fretted in her sleep. Shana instinctively swayed back and forth in a gentle rocking motion to soothe her, then lowered her voice as she spoke again. She definitely didn't want the other children or Carleen to hear her. "You know how those places are. No matter how good their reputation, it's a holiday weekend, staff will be minimal and everyone will wish they weren't there. We can't let her spend her first weekend without her parents in a situation like that!"

He arched one dark eyebrow. "We? I'm the social services director of this hospital and this is my decision, Ms. Devlin. Mine and Child Services. You have no say in the matter."

Desperation surged. "I'll take her home with me for the weekend," she blurted. "I don't mind. I have the weekend off."

Keith looked taken aback. "You…you can't do that."

"Why not?" A new burst of courage shored up her waning resolve. "I'm a certified day-care provider. Why can't I take her home for the weekend? I don't have any plans. I'll return her safely to you on Tuesday and then you can call Child Services."

He was shaking his head before she completed her last sentence. "Only a state-approved foster care giver or a member of the Child Services staff can take that child off the premises, Ms. Devlin."

She bit back a curse. "Don't we know anyone around here who's state approved?" Her first thought was Alexandra or maybe Carmen, the head teacher at Forrester Square Day Care.

He expelled a mighty breath. "There's no one, except me, of course. There's nothing—"

"You?" Disbelief struck Shana, almost knocking the wind out of her. "You're a state-approved foster care giver?"

He stared at her as if she should know the answer without asking, since he'd just told her. "Of course. It's a requirement for my position."

Shana felt better already. "Well, that settles it then. The baby can go home with you for the weekend." The idea quickly gained momentum. "After all, you were the first to care for her when she left the E.R. She'll likely remember your scent and the sound of your voice. That would work. She'd be happier with you than some stranger."

He was shaking that handsome head again. "That's not possible."

She strode across the room to stand toe-to-toe with him. "And why not?" She glared into those intense eyes without flinching. "Will it interfere with your personal plans? You can't give up the bachelor life-style for one weekend?" She shuddered—with revulsion, she told herself. It definitely couldn't be her proximity to him; she refused to believe he held that much power over her. "What kind of man are you that you'd put your sex life before the welfare of an innocent child? A helpless baby at that? I guess I was right. You aren't the fatherly type."

He glared right back at her, fury building in those mesmerizing amber eyes. "When did my sex life get involved with this?"

Her own rage took center court now. "You think I haven't heard about your exploits? I'm sure you have *big* plans for the weekend. Which nurse is it this time? The females around here all brag about how you…how you—''

''I get the picture.'' He cut her off, his voice gruff with his own escalating temper.

Shana struggled to regain control of herself. She'd let this whole conversation get out of hand. He'd really have reason to think her unprofessional now. She smoothed her fingers over the baby's fine blond hair, forcing herself to calm down. Shana wanted to cry at the loss this innocent little angel had suffered at barely one month old.

''Things are not as simple as that, Ms. Devlin,'' Keith said, his voice softer, as if he recognized her concern for what it was. As if he cared…

Shana looked up at him, hoping with all her heart that he'd make the decision to do the right thing. ''But it is simple. All you have to do is say yes.''

That relentless gaze of his locked with hers. For one long moment she was certain he planned to say no. Then he surprised her.

''Yes,'' he said, with something like amusement replacing the intensity in his eyes. ''I'll take the baby home with me for the weekend. On one condition,'' he qualified.

She waited expectantly, her heart doing a little somersault as she thanked God for his unexpected change of heart.

''I'll do it if you go, too.''

Shock quaked through her. Shana laughed, but the

sound held no humor. "If I'll go where?" she asked, certain she must have misunderstood.

"I'll take the baby home with me for the weekend if you come along, as well. No arguments, no compromises. I won't call Child Services until Tuesday."

Her eyelids fluttered rapidly to hide the clash of emotions she felt—shock, fear and something far too close to sensual heat. She backed up a step. "I'm not sure...." She wanted to. Damn it, she really did. But she shouldn't. Not for the reasons she felt simmering low in her belly right now. She hated the weakness he so easily instilled in her.

He tapped his watch. "It's your decision, but you're going to have to make it now."

Shana licked her lips nervously. Damn it all. It wasn't supposed to happen this way. She hated...okay, okay, she disliked the arrogant man. A little swirl of something far too close to desire funneled beneath her belly button. She brutally quashed the sensation. She would not be just another of Keith Hewitt's conquests. And it wasn't as if he was asking her out for a date. Which if he did, she promised herself, she would say no to without hesitation. Vanity made her long for the request, but good sense would prevail with a flat-out no. Wouldn't it?

"Fine," she agreed, relenting. He'd left her with no alternative. She would do what was best for the baby, regardless of her own needs or wants. And he definitely was not a part of anything she wanted or needed.

Another tiny whirl of delight curled through her tummy, making a liar out of her.

"I can leave early, since Carleen is here. I'll need to pick up some of my things first." She glared up at him with all the defiance she could rally. This was for the baby—nothing else.

"Fine," he echoed. "If you're ready, we'll leave as soon as I've spoken with Dr. Peters and Detective Dorsey."

"Why wouldn't I be ready?"

He held up a hand to fend off another round of dueling retorts. "Let's just do this."

"Okay," she muttered as she trailed after him. "Let's." All she needed was her purse and... The breadth of his shoulders snagged her attention; the air leaked from her lungs in one long whoosh. And a miracle. Otherwise, baby or no baby, she was going to find herself in bed with Seattle Memorial's most eligible bachelor.

And that simply would not do.

God, she was as bad as the rest of the females around here, and she was supposed to be immune.

In the corridor outside the nursery, Keith bumped into Annabelle Peters.

"I came as soon as I could," the doctor said quickly, and just as quickly averted her gaze.

She hadn't wanted to come, Keith realized, and he couldn't understand that. He'd asked her to meet him there. Her entire demeanor suddenly changed as Shana stepped out of the nursery, the baby in her arms. Keith refused to consider how natural she looked with a child nestled against her breast. It was her job, he reminded himself. This wasn't about anything else.

"May I?" Annabelle reached for the sleeping infant.

Shana smiled, and something inside Keith shifted. He looked away as she offered the child to Annabelle. What was it about Shana Devlin that could make him ache that way? It was late, he argued. He was exhausted.

And an idiot.

He couldn't believe he'd just issued such a foolish ultimatum. How could he spend the weekend with Shana?

For the baby.

No other reason.

This wasn't about anything else. He refused to believe the little wars they waged on a regular basis at the hospital meant anything other than the undeniable fact that they did not like each other. This had nothing to do with her representing a challenge. He was long past that sort of adolescent behavior.

Just then Jaron and his kids emerged from one of the rooms farther down the corridor.

Perfect timing, Keith decided. He would make this official all the way around. If it was official business, it couldn't be personal. "I need your okay on this," he said to Jaron.

The detective looked up, then frowned, his gaze landing squarely on Annabelle. Keith frowned, as well. What was it between those two? The sparks he'd noticed earlier came to mind…but it was more than mere sparks.

"Yours, too, Annabelle," Keith said, drawing her attention.

"What kind of okay?" Jaron inquired as he moved alongside Annabelle and peered down at the sleeping infant.

"I've decided to take the baby to the cabin with me for the weekend. With the holiday throwing a wrench in the usual protocol, we don't want her in some facility with strangers," he said, echoing Shana's words. "I'll call Child Services and get formal approval."

"You're doing this alone?" Annabelle sounded doubtful.

"Why?" Jaron asked promptly.

Keith tamped down his frustration and reminded himself that neither of them knew the whole story yet. "I'm registered as a foster parent, so it's completely legal."

Jaron looked as dubious as Annabelle. "But if she needs medical attention?"

"That's the beauty of it," Keith assured her. "Shana will be accompanying me to my cabin. She's had training as a nurse."

"That'll work." Annabelle looked at Shana. "I think that will be wonderful." She smiled wearily, her relief apparent. No one wanted the child to suffer.

Jaron still looked confused. "You don't have a problem with this arrangement?" he asked Annabelle.

When she shook her head, he looked even more confused.

"It's not the best arrangement for the child," she remarked, as casually as if they were discussing the weather. "Should relatives arrive, it will prove somewhat of an inconvenience, but it's a sound solution and meets the child's immediate needs."

"If anyone shows up from the family," Keith offered, "I'll have her back at the hospital in just over an hour. Since the car was stolen from somewhere close to the Canadian border, who knows how long it will take to locate next of kin?"

"Or even if they can be located," Annabelle added solemnly. "Shana is well-trained. She'll call for help if she needs it. Ben Jessup checked the infant out thoroughly. I don't see any reason not to agree to this."

Jaron looked thoughtful for a moment. "There was nothing in the diaper bag that might help in identification."

Keith shook his head. "I went through it again."

"And so did I," Shana added, shooting an annoyed look at Keith. "It only contained diapers, a couple of changes of clothes and formula. I was told the police have already itemized the contents and dusted it for prints but came up empty."

"I made a few calls and checked in with the station before I came down for the kids," Jaron said, almost as an afterthought.

It wasn't until then that Keith noticed the two small

children waiting quietly behind their father. Such good little soldiers, he thought sadly.

"There's nothing salvageable from the car," Jaron added, passing along what he'd learned.

Keith didn't like the sound of that. "So we wait until they're reported missing, is that what you're saying?"

"Yeah."

The group lapsed into defeated silence for a long moment. How would the baby fare in all this?

"You're okay with this?" Jaron suddenly asked Shana.

"I'm fine," she said in a clipped tone.

Keith started to demand why his friend would think otherwise, but Jaron lifted his daughter into his arms and said, "We'll be off."

How could Jaron drive with those hands? "Where's your car?" Keith could drive the detective and his kids home and then return to the hospital for Shana and the baby.

"At the station, but—"

Keith shook his head. "You're not driving with those hands."

"I'll catch a cab," Jaron countered, placing one hand atop his son's head as the little boy leaned against his leg.

"At nine o'clock on Friday night?" Keith held up his palms. "I don't think so. I'll take you and then come back for Shana and—"

"I'll drive you home."

The offer startled Keith as much as it clearly did

Jaron. Annabelle Peters offering to drive Jaron Dorsey home was about as unexpected as Keith inviting Shana to spend the weekend with him.

And that's exactly what he'd done. His gaze shifted to the woman who had been the bane of his existence since her arrival at Seattle Memorial.

And now there was no backing out, because the baby was counting on them.

His gaze moved to the infant still cradled lovingly in Annabelle's arms. The baby who'd lost her whole world in the space of a few hours. The baby who didn't have a name.

The mystery baby.

CHAPTER THREE

HE HAD LOST HIS MIND.

Keith had known it was coming. From the moment she'd hired on, every time he ran into Shana Devlin at the hospital, he did or said something unbelievably stupid. He couldn't quite pinpoint what it was, but there was something about her that unbalanced him. So he steered clear of her most of the time. Since Shana worked the night shift, avoiding her usually wasn't a problem.

Everyone at the hospital had noticed the way the two of them went head-to-head. They had nothing in common and appeared to live to torture each other. The connection was damn fierce. Still, he'd suspected it was only a matter of time before his libido overrode his good sense.

And now it had happened.

He'd taken the intensity to a new level, by inviting the woman to spend the weekend with him.

Sure, the baby would be there, but he had a bad feeling that wasn't going to stop the inevitable.

He had to stop it himself.

He had to be strong.

Shana Devlin was not his type. He liked his women

willing and submissive, and completely without strings. No doubt with a bit of prodding, Ms. Devlin might be willing enough, but he was quite sure she didn't have one submissive bone in her body. And he'd have to be blind not to recognize a woman who loved children, wanted children of her own soon. And before children came marriage.

Oh, he had nothing against marriage and children. The institution and the inevitable offspring produced just weren't in his five-year plan. At least, that's what he told himself every morning when he looked in the mirror…or when he had to call next of kin to pick up a newly orphaned child.

Some part of him had known that beneath the hostility lay much more powerful emotions. Emotions he wanted desperately to deny.

"You're sure you picked up everything she'll need?" Shana asked as she bent yet again to retrieve something from a bottom dresser drawer.

A couple of seconds passed before Keith could speak. The way her slacks molded her perfect derriere whenever she bent down made his trousers considerably less comfortable. He should never have started thinking about her body.

"I picked up everything on your list." He'd escorted Shana and the baby to her apartment so she could pack, while he went to the supercenter to pick up supplies the child would need for the weekend, including formula, diapers and a few extra changes of clothing.

Why wasn't Shana ready yet? He turned his back

and paced to the other side of the room. *Think about something else,* he commanded his irrational mind.

Her apartment was a one-room efficiency maintained by the hospital for staff. Except for a closet-size bathroom, the living room, kitchen, dining room and bedroom were all cramped into one space. One small space. But it was nice. He gave the room another slow sweep, anything to keep his eyes off her every move. The eclectic decorating reflected her spunky personality. The furnishings she'd selected were worn and comfortable and boasted a funky blend of new and old. The multicolored strands of beads hanging over the open doorway to her jam-packed closet jostled and clinked as she reached through them for another blouse.

Shana Devlin struck him as young, impulsive and far too eager for her own good. He supposed *spunky* did fit her. He'd heard the story of how she came to live in Seattle, and wondered what that said of her life in Iowa or Nebraska, or wherever she'd come from. Anyone who was ready to pull up roots and take off at the drop of a hat—well, that was simply odd in Keith's book. Alexandra Webber had provided her with a job, but that wasn't the point.

Shana Devlin had drifted here on a whim, like a gypsy who had no place to go except where the wind took her. That was precisely why he refused to acknowledge those underlying emotions where she was concerned. Stability was his motto. He needed it. Would never set himself up for anything less. Just one more reason to put off a permanent relationship.

"I guess I'm ready," she announced, snapping him back to the present.

She stood next to her bed, staring at him with a defiant tilt to her chin, as if she'd read his mind and didn't like what she'd found. Her short, wispy auburn hair hugged her face and throat in a way that was at once sexy and vulnerable. The silky material of the jade-green blouse she wore caressed her heavy breasts and slim torso, drawing his attention there. Black slacks shielded her long legs from his hungry gaze, and three suitcases sat at her feet.

Three?

Slack-jawed, he made a sound of disbelief. "We'll only be gone until Tuesday."

She quirked an auburn eyebrow. "I agreed to go— I didn't agree to go without the necessities of life."

Keith rolled his eyes heavenward and called himself every kind of fool. What on earth had he gotten himself into? He was already fighting a building arousal merely looking at her, and they hadn't even gotten to the cabin. They would be completely alone there, far from the social framework each used to keep distance between them. There would be nothing to stop them from… The baby.

Relief rushed out in a sigh.

The baby would have to be enough.

Shana stood there, calmly waiting for him to make the next move. Okay, he could do this. Everything would be fine. He glanced at the sleeping infant on her bed. Shana had placed a pillow on each side of her so she wouldn't roll off. That child was the only reason he was here, Keith reminded himself. They were both doing the right thing for the baby. There was no other motive involved.

"All right." He stormed up to Shana and lifted two of the suitcases. "I'll be back for the other one."

She reached down and hefted the remaining bag, inadvertently giving him an amazing view of her incredible cleavage. He swallowed hard. The woman had...well, very healthy breasts. She was tall and slender otherwise. But those breasts! He resisted the urge to set one of the suitcases down and tug at his collar. He was a leg man, though, he reminded himself. And since Shana Devlin always chose to wear slacks, he couldn't be sure what kind of legs she had. He consoled himself with the certainty that her legs would likely be a huge disappointment. His gaze roved the length of those long limbs once more. Doubt replaced his certainty.

"I'll set this one out in the hallway," she offered.

He nodded, mostly because he couldn't speak at the moment. He was too caught up in the internal war over which he preferred most, breasts or legs, and her possible inadequacy where the latter was concerned. Either way, he had a dreadful feeling that he was doomed.

Once he'd loaded her luggage and she'd followed with the sleeping infant, strapped into the car seat they'd borrowed from the hospital, they were ready. Baby Chris, as Shana insisted on calling her, was safely tucked in the center position of the back seat. The woman shredding his control with every breath she took relaxed into the front passenger seat with a throaty sigh, as if she'd never before sat in luxuriously padded leather seats.

Keith climbed behind the wheel of his SUV and offered his adult passenger a tight smile. "It'll take us about an hour to get to my cabin. Go ahead and get some sleep if you'd like. I don't need any company to stay awake." He didn't want to hear her voice…hell, he didn't even want to hear her breathe.

She stretched like a cat, her spine arching, those plump breasts jutting forward, making his mouth water. "That would be nice." She combed her fingers through her short, silky hair and glanced at the digital clock on the dash. "Gosh, it's almost midnight."

He grunted a response, his brain too busy doing instant replays of that lithe body stretching…of those fabulous breasts thrusting forward…of the way tendrils of auburn hair caressed her long neck.

"Is something wrong?" she asked, those expressive brown eyes studying him closely.

Shaking off his lecherous thoughts, he forced himself to face forward. "No." He cleared his throat of its huskiness. "I'm fine. Everything's fine." He started the engine and shifted into Drive.

"Good," she said slumberously. "I can't wait to get to bed."

SLOWLY SHANA BECAME AWARE that the vehicle had stopped, but precisely what that meant didn't sink all the way through the haze of sleep still shrouding her. The sound of rain pattering on the windshield made her want to snuggle up and sleep forever. When she attempted to do just that, the delicate squeak of buttery-soft leather made her eyes flutter open.

Where was she?

It was dark. A light drizzle was falling. She squinted but could see nothing beyond the rivulets of water slipping down the glass.

"Use my jacket to protect the baby from the rain."

That voice…

Shana's head came up.

Keith Hewitt.

She was in his car.

She turned just in time to have his elegant navy jacket thrust at her.

Oh God.

This was a mistake.

With a shaky hand she accepted the jacket. The feel of it, as well as the scent that belonged exclusively to him, immediately overwhelmed her senses.

"Where are we?" she managed to ask without her voice quavering.

"My cabin. Near Cedar Creek."

The cabin. Oh, yeah.

She peered through the rain-streaked glass once more and made out the dark shapes…trees, lots of them.

If she remembered her geography, they were basically in the middle of nowhere and still only an hour or so from the city.

"I'll get the last of the luggage. I've already unlocked the door and carried in a couple of bags."

She shivered. From the cool air floating in through his open door, she assured herself. It wasn't his voice. Or the jacket she'd unconsciously hugged to her chest. Shana gave herself a little shake. *Snap out of it,* she ordered. Nothing was going to happen during the next seventy-two hours spent alone with this man. No way. She didn't care how fantastic the other women at the hospital claimed Keith Hewitt was in and out of bed.

Shana had no intention of getting to know him that well in either situation.

She scrambled between the seats and climbed into the back to sit next to Baby Chris, who still slept.

As she lifted the infant from the car seat into her arms, Shana cooed and whispered baby talk to her.

Instinctively inhaling Keith's scent, she cloaked his jacket around the precious bundle. Her stomach quivered at the idea that he'd had the foresight to offer his jacket to cover the baby. Maybe she was wrong about the guy. Maybe he wasn't just a macho jerk who used his job to further his sex life.

Her dash into the log cabin didn't allow for a survey of the terrain or even the place she would call home for the next few days. She scarcely had time to note that it was, indeed, log-and-chink construction, and that utter stillness and silence surrounded it. The only sound was the rain filtering through the heavy canopy of trees.

Once inside, she swiped a few drops of rain from her cheeks and laid Keith's jacket on the closest chair, uncovering the fretting infant. Chris didn't like having her face covered. After rhythmically patting the baby's bottom and snuggling her close to calm her uneasiness, Shana surveyed the decor.

It was rustic, but not too much so. The sofa and accompanying chairs were brown leather and worn to softness. The tables were knotty pine, like the floors. The numerous windows were uncluttered by draperies or blinds, just another indication of the solitude that no doubt surrounded the place. A vaulted ceiling soared upward, displaying lovely beams and a second-story landing. The living room, kitchen and dining room took up most of the downstairs floor space, and a narrow hall disappeared into the darkness at the rear of the house. She supposed it led to a back door or laundry room, or both.

Keith appeared on the upstairs landing. "Come on up and I'll show you your room."

For one long moment she couldn't move. She could only stare at the vision he made, poised against that rustic wood railing. His tie hung loosely at his open collar, where he'd already unfastened a couple of buttons. The white shirt was wet, making it nearly transparent, and it was plastered to him like a second skin. That dark, wavy hair looked disheveled, just begging to have fingers run through it.

He hitched a thumb over his shoulder. "Your luggage and the stuff for the baby are already up here."

She nodded mutely, emerging from the coma she'd fallen victim to.

Holding the baby like a shield in front of her, she climbed the stairs. Over and over in her head she chanted the mantra that would save her: *He's a jerk...self-centered...uncaring about anything but furthering his career.* He probably didn't like kids. Considering the way he'd held the baby, he didn't even like being around them. This whole deal could be nothing more than a devious plan to conquer the one woman at the hospital who didn't swoon at his charms.

He intended to have her, just to prove he could.

All the considerate things he did like offering his jacket to protect the baby from the rain, were most likely part of a well-planned strategy to touch her where he knew she was the most vulnerable. Shana loved children. Wanted at least two of her own. Somehow Keith Hewitt understood that about her and planned to use the whole mystery-baby thing to his advantage.

Anger boiled up inside her. Well, let him give it his best shot. She was onto him. He'd thrown her for a loop at first, but she was on the same page with him now.

He would fail.

When she reached the landing, her gaze narrowed. Oh, yes. She had his number, all right. And he was going to be sorely disappointed by his inability to conquer the only woman who didn't fall at his feet.

Shana smiled.

And she was going to enjoy every minute of making him feel inadequate. A plan quickly took shape in her mind. He wasn't the only one who could do a little conquering. Maybe she'd teach this Casanova what it felt like to be on the receiving end of devious designs.

A frown marred his features as she came nearer. "Is everything all right?"

Shana smiled sweetly. "Everything's wonderful. You have a great place." She glanced appreciatively down at the first floor. "Just lovely."

He nodded uncertainly, as if suspicious of her compliment. He was very perceptive. She'd have to be careful or he'd figure out what she was up to.

"I'd better get the baby settled," she suggested, keeping her pleasant smile in place despite her desire to shout that she knew exactly what he was up to and he could just forget it right now.

He led her to the first door on the right of the short upstairs hall. "The room has a private bath. If you don't find everything you need, let me know."

Shana nodded, the movement strained. This close to him, she found it impossible to keep her mind fixed on her goal. The sweet smell of rain had mixed with his unique male scent and was now blocking the neuron pathways of reason between her brain and her body. Heat pumped inside her, making her feel restless and needy. All she had to do, she told herself, was sidle past him and close the door behind her. When she'd had more sleep she could better deal with the blatant sexuality he exuded—an appeal that drew her like a beacon in the night.

"Good night," he said, that deep voice low and soothing as she squeezed past him in the open doorway.

She stalled, her gaze going to his. "Good night," she murmured past the tightening in her throat. Her smile drooped considerably. *Please,* she prayed, *just let him go.*

But he didn't. Instead, he inclined that handsome head and peered down at the infant in her arms with a soft chuckle. "I can't believe she slept through all this."

Shana reminded herself this had to be a trick. He wanted her soft, pliable. She would not surrender.

"I'd like to get some sleep myself," she said, and moved fully into the room. Before that carnal mouth could utter another word, she closed the door in his face.

Shana blew out the breath she'd been holding and sagged with relief. She shuddered at the receding emotions he so easily engendered in her. This weekend was about the baby, nothing else. All she had to do was remember that.

Using an extra blanket she found in the closet and the largest drawer the bureau offered, she quickly arranged a bed for Chris. After feeding and changing and a few minutes of cuddling, the baby slept soundly once more. Shana placed her in the makeshift crib and drew back the covers of her own bed, but decided against climbing in immediately.

The bedroom was not large, but it was nicely furnished and had a cozy feel about it. A set of French doors suggested that perhaps a balcony overlooked the back of the property, but the rain still falling outside kept her from verifying that. Still too wired to sleep, she decided to put her things away. It wasn't until she'd taken a closer look at the closet and the bathroom that she realized this had to be Keith's room. Goose bumps rose on her skin. He'd obviously taken the smaller of the two bedrooms and forgone the private bath in deference to her comfort.

She clenched her jaw. She would not give him any points for being hospitable. Anyone would have done the same. The gesture didn't make him special.

After brushing her teeth and changing into a nightshirt, Shana crawled between the welcoming sheets. She snuggled into the soft covers and sighed contentedly. God, she was tired. All she wanted to do was sleep.

In Keith's bed.

Her eyes popped open and her body tensed.

Had he changed the linens since his last visit?

Shana flung off the covers and huffed in exasperation. Well, there went any chance of getting a moment's rest. How could she sleep, when all she wanted to do was imagine the ways he'd lain in this very bed? Had he made love here with one of his numerous conquests?

She squeezed her eyes shut and counted backward from one thousand. There had to be a way to block the man from her thoughts. Had to be a way to rid herself of the mental images plaguing her.

Twenty minutes later she admitted defeat and snuggled back under the covers. Shana drifted off to sleep and dreamed of making love with the man down the hall. In her dreams it was everything she'd known it would be...and more.

SOMETHING WOKE HIM just as the sun crept above the treetops. Keith stirred, rolled over and groaned. He'd only been asleep a short while. Getting up now was definitely not something he wanted to do. He needed to sleep.

She had kept him awake for hours after he'd gone to bed.

As if the mere thought of Shana was all it took to blast the last vestiges of sleep from his weary body, his eyes flew open and his heart picked up an extra twenty beats per minute.

She was here.

In his room.

Less than ten yards from where he lay, his eyes burning from lack of sleep, his body hard with need and—

The sounds that had disturbed his restless sleep filtered through his ruminations.

Shana's voice, weak and broken. And an infant wailing like a siren.

Keith sat bolt upright in bed.

He swore and threw the covers back.

The baby!

And the woman who'd plagued him since—

"Keith!" Shana cried out again, her voice weak and quavering.

He sprang from the bed, jerked on his trousers and rushed from his room.

Her door was still closed, but the baby's insistent cries easily penetrated the barrier.

He didn't bother to knock, just opened the door and burst into the room.

From her makeshift bed on the floor, the baby cried, her little face red, her arms and legs flailing.

"Keith," Shana whimpered from the bathroom.

He looked from the baby to the open bathroom door and back. Confusion ruled for about five seconds. With no other choice, he picked up the infant and headed toward the door. The baby wriggled in his arms, her whole body shuddering with her rising sobs.

Shana sat on the floor near the toilet. She'd sagged against the wall, as if holding herself upright was an impossible task. She looked drawn and pale. She looked…ill.

Dread pooled in his gut.

"What's wrong?" Desperation tinged his tone. Every instinct told him that no matter what she said, it wouldn't be good.

Those wide brown eyes opened. She moistened her lips and looked entirely miserable. "I'm sick."

When he started toward her, she held up a hand. "Don't bring the baby in here."

He took a step backward.

"What's wrong?" The baby had calmed a little, but his own heart had taken up the slack. It pounded beneath his sternum like a racehorse headed down the final stretch to the finish line.

"I don't know if I ate something last night that disagreed with me or if it's a bug of some sort." Shana pressed a hand to her stomach and moaned softly.

"What…what can I do to help?"

She swept a silky tendril of hair from her forehead. "Nothing right now. Just take care of the baby. She's hungry."

Take care of the baby.

He stared at the squirming infant in his arms. Fear gripped him by the throat. He couldn't do that. He'd never…

"What am I supposed to do?" His desperation had morphed into outright panic.

"The formula is the ready-mixed kind. Put some in a bottle and feed her. It's simple." Shana swallowed, her hand still pressed to her abdomen. "Then change her diaper and she'll probably go right back to sleep."

Probably? Keith shook his head. "But I don't know how to…"

Baby Chris let out a howl that would not be denied. Keith stiffened. Was he doing something wrong? Holding her too tightly? Not tightly enough?

"Feed her," Shana said wearily. "And stay away from this room. I just hope it's nothing contagious."

She looked so fragile. Keith felt torn between rushing to feed the baby and helping Shana in some way.

"You're sure you don't need anything? A doctor?"

She shook her head. "Just go. I'll be okay."

Keith backed away from the door.

He looked down at the infant in his arms once more.

How in the world was he supposed to do this?

He had absolutely no experience taking care of children on this level. The paperwork was one thing. Even strong-arming some bureaucrat or health care professional into doing what was best for a patient was a piece of cake. But he'd never, ever had to feed, diaper or pacify a crying baby.

That's why he'd brought Shana along. At least that's what he'd told himself…and it was true to an extent. Confessing to anything else at the moment would be pointless.

His plans had backfired.

And he had no choice but to do what had to be done.

He swallowed back the fear burgeoning in his throat. "Okay, kid," he said to the baby. "Let's go find some chow."

CHAPTER FOUR

SHANA HAD BEEN RIGHT. A few minutes after he'd fed the baby, she was asleep. He set the empty bottle aside and stared down at the tiny infant in his arms. Something shifted deep inside Keith's chest.

She was all alone in the world…at least for now. Her mother and father were gone—just like his. A frown inched across his brow as he considered the reality of the situation. This child would have no memory of her parents. Not a single moment of recall as to what her mother or father looked like, the sound of their voices, or anything else. A new wave of sadness swamped him, made his chest tighten and ache. That, he decided, was the worst of all.

At least he had memories of his mother, and certainly decades of fond moments with his father, who'd died just last year. Keith thought for a moment about his mom. He'd been only a boy at the time, but he remembered well the smell of cookies. She'd baked the absolute best peanut butter cookies. The scent would fill the house. He closed his eyes and summoned the smell that was forever imprinted in his memory. God, he hadn't had home-baked cookies in forever.

He forced his eyes open and banished that sentimental line of thinking. He didn't need anyone in his life on that level. Going out on an emotional limb was only asking for trouble, asking for pain. He'd had enough for two lifetimes. There wasn't a reason on earth worth the risk.

Instantly, as if to refute his conclusion, the image of Shana Devlin clad only in an apron and lifting freshly baked treats from a cookie sheet filled his mind. She would offer him a taste and he would accept. Except in this fantasy, it wasn't the cookies that filled his hungry mouth. It was her ripe, succulent breasts, first one and then the other. He imagined her taste, soft and subtle, but more erotic than anything he'd ever encountered.

A crisp burp startled him from his musings. He stared down at the baby still clutched in his arms, and almost jumped in surprise. He'd forgotten to burp her, though she had, apparently, done all right on her own. How could his overactive imagination go from baby to memories of his mom to...*that* in a mere instant?

Keith shook his head. He had to be losing his mind.

Surging to his feet, he forced himself to review the situation in a more realistic manner. He had a job to do. He carefully placed Baby Chris in the nest of blankets he'd arranged on the sofa and scooted a ladder-back chair in close so she wouldn't roll off.

He nodded approvingly at his own ingenuity. Shana wasn't the only one who could properly care for the child. Perhaps he hadn't needed her, after all.

Instinct warned him that was not the case. Surviving one feeding without incident was not the same as making it through the whole weekend. He had no way of knowing how often Shana had been required to get up and attend to the child while he'd slept.

Well, he hadn't slept all that much. He'd spent most of the hours before dawn tossing and turning and living fantasy after fantasy about the woman sleeping in his bed. Fantasies like the one he'd just experienced.

Keith shook himself to force away the images that continued to filter into his thoughts. He had to stay on track here. This weekend was about the baby, not about hot sex with the one woman who drove him mad most of the time.

Only then did he stop to consider that he'd dragged on his trousers from last night and could definitely use a shower. He looked at the child sleeping so peacefully, her tiny lips puckered in an instinctive sucking motion.

He certainly couldn't leave the baby here while he went upstairs to shower.

With no other recourse, he moved the chair aside and scooped the soft bundle into his arms, thankfully without rousing the slumbering angel.

Upstairs, Keith hesitated outside Shana's room and listened for a moment. When several seconds elapsed without a sound, he moved on. Hopefully, she was asleep. From the look of her, she'd gotten less rest than he had. Not to mention that she was clearly very ill. He made up his mind then and there. If she wasn't noticeably better when he checked on her next, he was calling a doctor.

Things could go downhill far too quickly to take chances. The memory of his mother came to him unbidden. One day she'd been fine, baking cookies and doing laundry, and the next she'd been on her deathbed.

He forced away the recollection and concentrated on the present. Jaron would find someone to take the child as soon as he identified the family. As Keith placed Baby Chris on the bed and positioned a pillow on each side of her, the way he'd seen Shana do, he made the infant a silent promise. She would not be thrust into foster care with strangers if there was a single living relative willing and able to care for her. Keith would see to it…just as his good friend Jaron would.

That was what made Seattle Memorial different from most large hospitals. The staff really cared, on a level that transcended the norm. It was this caring that kept him in Seattle. Well, there was also the fact that he and his father had immensely enjoyed their weekends at this cabin. Though Keith no longer had any family of his own, he had the hospital. He had his friends and his work. He had his occasional weekends here. That was enough.

As if to refute that conclusion, Shana's smile invaded his senses. It wasn't just the way she looked. It was the way she smelled, the creaminess of her skin and, loath though he was to admit it, the lyrical sound of her voice. Not when she was speaking to him, of course, but when she spoke to the children.

Her devotion to children was undeniable; he would give her that. It was in other areas that they went head-to-head. Just the other day in the cafeteria she'd overheard him mention who he planned to support in the next presidential race. Of course, Shana supported the other party and had let him know it.

Every muscle in his body tensed when he thought of how she clearly adored challenging his every word. It was as if she had something to prove, and had decided he would be the testing ground.

Ordering himself to relax, he gathered the day's attire—jeans and a flannel shirt—then, pausing to check the baby once more, headed across the hall.

With a final glance toward Shana's door to see that it was firmly closed, he entered the bathroom, leaving the door open so that he would hear the baby if she awoke. He'd make this shower his fastest ever, he decided, as he stripped off his trousers and stepped beneath the spray of water before it had heated to the desired temperature.

The cool water sluiced over him, raising bumps on his skin but, unbelievably, doing nothing to lessen his rigid condition below the waist.

How was it the mere thought of the woman could keep him in a perpetual state of semiarousal even when she looked like hell and was probably ill with something they would all suffer before the weekend was through?

He had no answer for the question.
Only time would tell.

SHANA WOKE AROUND 10:00 a.m.

She rolled onto her side and peered at the digital clock on the bedside table, then relaxed on her back once more.

Lying there, she took stock of herself. She had a sleep hangover. She rarely slept past eight, even when she worked late. Her stomach felt okay…not great, but definitely better than it had a few hours ago. She had no fever, no headache or other symptom that would suggest a virus.

She was convinced now that it had been the lasagna she'd scarfed down in the hospital cafeteria last night. The cafeteria's food was usually very good, but she had a feeling it was more the ravenous way she'd consumed it rather than the food itself that had made her stomach rebel. And then there was Keith Hewitt. She'd been totally unnerved by the whole episode last night. The poor sweet baby who'd lost her parents. Keith's demand that she accompany him if he was to keep the child for the weekend. Annabelle's odd behavior regarding the child's mother. Jaron Dorsey's intensity where Annabelle was concerned.

The whole shooting match was strange and definitely enough to upset one's constitution.

Shana pushed herself up on her elbows and listened intently.

Nothing.

Where was the baby?

Asleep?

Her curiosity—or perhaps worry—propelled her from the bed. She threaded her fingers through her hair in a futile effort to give some order to it, and tiptoed out into the hallway.

She stopped, listening again. Still nothing.

When she started toward the staircase, she heard it.

Soft murmuring…

A shiver went straight through her as she identified the sounds.

Keith's voice.

Downstairs.

She edged toward the railing that overlooked the great room below. Holding her breath so as not to make a sound, she peered down at the scene.

Barefoot, Keith slowly paced the hardwood floor. His fancy suit had been replaced by a red-checked flannel shirt, with the tails left hanging haphazardly around his jeans. The image was so unlike the man she was accustomed to seeing at the hospital in his designer suits and ties. But there was something wrong with the shirt. It was…

A smile spread across her lips. It was buttoned wrong, as if he'd been in a hurry.

Then the sound started again. Her heart stuttered to a near stop. Keith was singing softly to the infant. Shana strained to hear, deciding the song was something like ''Hush, Little Baby.'' But it wasn't the tune or the words she could scarcely make out that made her heart pitch into a sudden acrobatic act. It was the whole picture.

Dark chestnut waves fell across Keith's forehead as he peered down at the infant. His deep voice sounded both tender and sexy as he sang softly. Baby Chris fretted a moment longer, then seemed to settle.

But Keith didn't immediately leave off his ministrations. Instead, he paced, one hand rhythmically patting the baby's bottom as he hummed a few more notes.

It was then that Shana recognized the absolute precariousness of her situation. Keith had not offered her his coat to protect the baby when they arrived simply to make her think he was kind. Or maybe he had. But she seriously doubted it. He had no idea she was watching at this moment. That he would sing to the baby, of all things, gave her a smidgen of insight into the man.

He did care about the child.

This weekend was likely about the infant, not his overblown ego and the need to take down the final holdout of the hospital's female staff.

Maybe she'd been wrong about him all along.

Maybe he was just a nice guy who liked women.

Lots of women.

Ire kindled low in her belly. He dated a different woman almost every week. Broke countless hearts. Never committed.

No, she was right about him. No way could she be that wrong.

He was a Casanova. He used his God-given assets and anything else required to accomplish his goals. She'd heard all about his sweet-talking ways.

Her mother had warned her about good-looking men. And her mother had known firsthand the heartache they could cause. Shana's own father had sought the comfort of another woman. God rest his soul. Her mother had despised him for the weakness. She'd sworn that good-looking men were only a source of pain.

Shana definitely was not going to follow the same path as her mother. Yes, she wanted a husband and a family of her own. A real family that belonged to her. She loved Alexandra and definitely considered her family, and of course she had her brother, Brett. Still, there was something about having her *own* family that appealed to her on every level. She wanted it so very much.

But she would not suffer what her mother had suffered to have it. She would not fall in love with a charmer like Keith. A man who moved from woman to woman the same way he went through shirts.

No, she refused to take that kind of risk.

Her body heated and shivered at Keith's next move. She cursed her traitorous reactions and turned away from the sight of him pressing a sweet kiss to the baby's forehead.

Obviously, in this environment, she had no objectivity where the man was concerned. At the hospital it was easy to hate him, to throw daggers and walk away. But here…

She slowed in her retreat to his bedroom. This was his territory. Personal territory that reeked of pure male dominance. Even the baby's presence wasn't enough to ensure that she kept her distance.

It was time to fall back on plan A. Shana resumed her journey, a new confidence in her step. There was only one way to fight this kind of fire.

With fire.

She wasn't about to slip into Keith's trap. Not when she could set a trap of her own. She hadn't missed how unsettled he was by her forwardness whenever they argued a point. If she concentrated on making him uneasy, that would keep her distracted from the way he made her feel. She could watch him squirm.

And all the while she would keep her goal firmly in mind.

Show Keith Hewitt what it was like to be prey instead of the predator.

She could do it.

It would be easy.

In the en suite bathroom she twisted the shower knobs and waited for the water to warm. Well, maybe it wouldn't be easy. She considered the way his mere touch—or even just a glance—made her feel. But she could do it. She would always look back on this weekend with fond memories and know that she had accomplished two very important things.

One, she'd kept Baby Chris safe and happy.

Two, she'd given Keith Hewitt a taste of his own medicine.

After she'd showered, Shana reviewed what she'd brought with her. She always prepared well. Growing up, she hadn't been a Girl Scout or anything, but she had learned the hard way that the ill-prepared person lived to regret it. Her mother had been famous for impromptu family outings, usually related to getting away from one of her father's suspected indiscretions.

Shana had brought along several changes of clothes, mostly jeans and pullover blouses for comfort. She'd packed her cosmetics, though she rarely wore anything more than blush and lip gloss. Everything she needed for styling her hair—dryer, gel, her favorite brush. A couple of nighties—the one she'd slept in last night, which was nothing more than an oversize shirt, and something a bit more feminine—spaghetti straps, silk. The latter had been an afterthought, she had to admit.

Or maybe it hadn't. Maybe she'd subconsciously thrown in a few teasing garments. The silky underwear was pretty much the only kind she owned. It was her one self-indulgence. She loved the feel of fine silk against her skin, and the racier the style, the better.

She glared at her reflection in the mirror. Okay, it was her one secret weakness. She liked sexy undies. What did it matter, anyway? No one ever saw them.

Shana sighed. Enough with the pity session.

She dabbed a little gloss on her lips. It wasn't that she didn't get asked out. She did. And she wasn't some naive virgin. She'd had a couple of experiences.

A long time ago, she admitted with a shrug.

A really long time ago, a little voice echoed, making her cringe.

Okay, back in high school had been the first time. She made a face and relegated the perfectly awful incident to the farthest recesses of her mind. Then there was that three-month relationship in nursing school. It hadn't been so bad, but somehow she'd come out on the short end of the stick. The intimate side of the relationship had never really done anything for her.

So maybe she was the problem.

Shana stilled. Maybe that's why Keith never asked her out, the way he did every other living female under forty on the hospital staff.

She was pretty enough, she argued as she stared at her reflection. Not beautiful, but cute. Her body was a little ill-proportioned—big breasts, but almost too thin everywhere else. She shrugged. There was nothing she could do about that. She'd inherited her figure from her mother. Maybe it was the glasses she wore for paperwork, she thought, desperate for a plausible explanation. She supposed she did look a little prudish in them.

But there were other women on staff who wore glasses, and at least two of them had been out with Keith.

She tugged on her blouse self-consciously, adjusting it so that it reached the waist of her jeans. Maybe she didn't give off the right signals. She'd never really thought about it before. She just did what she did best—took care of children.

When she hadn't been able to tolerate the life-and-death roller-coaster ride associated with nursing, she'd turned to early childhood education, thinking she might like to teach. Then her mother had grown ill, and Shana had taken care of her until she passed away. Though Shana had finished her education, she'd missed out on job offerings for the new school year. The only offer that had come along was at the Labor of Love Child Development Center in her hometown. She'd accepted the position and found her true calling—taking care of children.

She loved her work. Was quite good at it, if she did say so herself. She'd likely still be at Labor of Love if Alexandra Webber hadn't come into her life. The promise of an equivalent position and a new adventure had brought Shana to Seattle.

She tidied the bathroom and went to make her bed. It wasn't that her life had been boring back home, but with her mother's death and her brother's preoccupation with work, she had felt kind of...lonesome. The idea that her stepfather and new stepsister awaited her here in Seattle had been more than she could resist. She'd decided that a fresh start would be good for the personal slump she'd fallen into. Not unlike her dear brother, Shana had found herself consumed by work. She'd had no life outside the center, and that was not a good thing. She couldn't understand how Brett could handle it.

She needed people around her, in her life. She needed a relationship!

Smoothing a hand over the striped comforter, Shana sighed with abject disgust. She was young enough that she shouldn't be hearing her biological clock ticking so darn loudly. It wasn't time yet! Thirty was years away. And nowadays, even being well beyond thirty was no hindrance to marriage and child-bearing. She had oodles of time!

Collapsing onto the side of the bed, she rested her chin in her hand and huffed out an exasperated breath. So why did it feel as though time was running out, rushing past her like sand sifting between her fingers? It had to be that she still missed her mother, and of course, not a day went by that she didn't wish with all her heart that Brett was closer.

Alex was getting married in the spring. Maybe all the talk about weddings and bridal magazines was the reason for Shana's melancholy.

Taking a deep breath, she pushed herself to her feet. Well, whatever the reason, she wasn't going to mope around. She had a baby to look after and a man to teach a lesson to.

With that last thought firmly in place, she went downstairs to set the first lesson in motion.

By Tuesday, Keith Hewitt would have a whole new respect for the game of love.

KEITH CAREFULLY TUCKED the baby into her make-shift bed on the sofa and glanced up just in time to catch Shana descending the staircase.

"Thank God," he murmured as he slid the chair into place in front of the sofa.

Though the baby hadn't really been that much trouble, he was relieved that Shana was back in form so that she could take over. He just didn't feel equipped to handle the possibilities.

"You're looking much better," he said congenially

as he moved toward her. His smile came of its own accord, mainly because his gaze quickly took in the fit of her jeans as well as the swell of her breasts beneath the snug blouse. Hers was definitely a form to be savored. He resisted the urge to shake his head. Why did he always think like that whenever she was around?

"I feel much better, thank you," she said quietly as she regarded him with something akin to disdain.

His smile dimmed and his confusion gained momentum. "If you feel up to eating, there are still a few pancakes left."

Those brown eyes widened in surprise. "You cooked?"

Offended that she would think him incapable, he countered, "Well, yes. How else would I eat?" What did she think single men did? Order out all the time? This was the twenty-first century. Men could cook and still be *men*.

She seemed at a loss for words. "Of—of course," she stammered. "You're right. I guess I just thought…" The words trailed off, but the innuendo hung in the air like a ghost that refused to go away.

"That I wasn't capable of the task?" he suggested.

She'd hit a nerve, Shana realized. Fury was etched in every feature of his handsome face. Shana turned up her palms in a helpless gesture. "I don't know. I guess the idea just doesn't fit with my image of you."

"Like the concept of fatherhood didn't fit?"

Uh-oh. She'd only dug herself in deeper. Backing toward the kitchen, she hastened to assure him, "We can discuss this later. Right now—'' she pressed a hand to her tummy ''—I'd like to eat and see if things are back in working order.''

She turned and walked quickly in the direction of the wonderful smell. Skirting the island that separated the kitchen from the rest of the large room, she quickly scanned the countertop, then opened the oven door and inhaled deeply. The smell of freshly made pancakes had her moaning with pleasure.

''At least you're better,'' he said from right behind her.

Shana jumped, inadvertently coming face-to-face with him before quickly taking a step back. ''Yes, I think so.''

He stared down at her, those lionlike amber eyes questioning. ''I could use some more sleep if you're prepared to take over watching the baby.''

She started to say yes, but something stopped her. No, she didn't want him rested. She wanted him on edge. She wanted him pushed to the limit. A pleased smile stretched across her face before she could stop it. Biting her lower lip, she adopted a look of concern.

''That would be okay,'' she offered, ''except I can't be sure it's safe…'' her gaze locked with his ''…just yet.''

Only then did she notice the lines of fatigue marring those magnificent features. Before, she'd been too taken with his irritation at her remark—or maybe with that handsome face in general. But now she saw the reality. He was tired. As she watched, he plowed a hand through his hair, shoving all those dark, wavy strands away from his face. Her heart, traitorous organ that it was, foolishly skipped a beat.

She felt her resolve weakening. There was really no doubt in her mind that she was fine. She should let him get some sleep.

No way.

This opportunity might never come again. She had to teach him a lesson. For his own good…and for all those women whose hearts he'd broken.

"I'm feeling better." She shrugged. "I don't have a fever. But I really think we should give it a few hours and make sure no other symptoms are going to pop up before I take over care of the baby." She reached for the pancakes and offered an apologetic smile. "Just in case."

"Fine."

He started to turn away but she stopped him. "Wait."

She set the pancakes on the island counter and turned back. "You're all wrong," she said innocently.

A frown of confusion marred his brow. "What do you mean?"

He so hated being accused of anything less than perfection. Maybe that was why she loved to argue with everything he said. He was so completely certain he was right. Always right. A know-it-all. It was past time he was taken down a notch or two.

"You've missed a button," she explained as she reached for his shirt.

Before he could react and step out of her reach, as

she fully expected him to do, she'd undone the first button. Then the second. He didn't move, didn't argue, just stood very still as she slipped button after button from its closure.

When she reached the last one, she glanced up, intending to tease him, but the look in his eyes stole away her breath and any possibility of speech.

Suddenly Shana wished she was wearing her glasses, for some other kind of shield against what she saw there—desire, hot and ravenous.

He wanted her.

The truly scary thing was, she wanted him, too.

She moistened her lips to say something, anything. But the certainty that he was going to kiss her and that she was going to let him rendered her mute.

That carnal mouth lowered slowly toward hers. As if on cue, she lifted her chin, putting their lips in better alignment for the meeting that was to come.

A cry pierced the tension.

Two beats passed before either of them moved.

"The baby," he murmured, echoing Shana's thought exactly.

And just like that, it was over.

CHAPTER FIVE

FEELING GUILTY FOR HER deception, Shana decided the least she could do was tidy up a bit. Keith, fabulous pancake maker though he might be, was quite a messy cook. She'd never seen so much flour tossed about on countertops, or spilled milk. She wondered who'd stocked the refrigerator and cabinets. She'd checked them all and was considerably impressed by the bounty.

Maybe he stayed here more often than she'd first thought. She surveyed the cabin in a different light. Maybe this was his bachelor lair.

But then, it didn't fit the ''smooth Casanova'' image she'd associated with Keith.

The setting and the cabin were rustic. Though the place was located only an hour from the busy streets of Seattle, there was a quiet solitude here. Lots and lots of trees. It was a great getaway, she had to admit. Just not one she would have pictured Keith enjoying with his female of the week.

After cleaning up the kitchen area, she wandered around the great room. Rather than a deer head or something equally macho, a vine-and-pinecone wreath hung over the fireplace's massive mantel. A few framed photographs stood proudly among the other mementos there. She studied the pictures and decided the older man in each had to be Keith's father. The two looked very much alike. One photo in particular caught her eye; the matching smiles captured in it were nearly breathtaking. The two men, fishing poles in hand, stood side by side near a creek in the woods. Shana wondered if that creek was nearby. Perhaps this cabin was their special place.

She rolled her eyes and propped her hands on her hips. There she went again, giving Keith the benefit of the doubt. First the cabin was his lair for sexual rendezvous, then it was the special place he and his father shared.

What a nitwit she was. She could stand here and presume anything she wanted to, but her mother had always said that actions spoke louder than words. Shana knew what she saw every day at the hospital. Keith Hewitt was a lady's man. He was not husband and father material in any shape, form or fashion.

She would not be fooled by him.

Speaking of which, where was he?

He'd disappeared with the baby. He hadn't gone up the stairs, she was certain.

Peeking out the front door, she saw the SUV they had arrived in and little else except trees. Thankfully, all signs of the rain had vanished and the sun was shining.

She should find him and see if he had everything under control. The memory of that near kiss zoomed into vivid 3-D focus. On second thought, maybe she'd better steer clear of him for a while. She chewed her bottom lip. But there was the baby to consider. She couldn't be sure Keith really knew what he was doing when it came to child care.

Her mind made up, Shana went in search of her shoes, then hurried out the front door. Whatever lesson she decided to teach Keith, her first priority was the baby. She'd had her fun this morning making him suffer a while longer, but it was time to get back to business now.

To say she was startled when she found the driveway empty would be a vast understatement. The SUV had been there just minutes ago. She'd seen it.

Her heart started to pound. What if something had happened? What if the baby was sick and Keith had decided to drive her to the hospital without taking the time to find Shana? Surely he wouldn't just leave without telling her…

She ran all the way around the cabin, finding nothing but more woods. Her mind raced with possibilities. God, what she would give for a cell phone. But what good would it do her? She didn't know if Keith had one, and she didn't know his number anyway.

This was her payback for behaving so selfishly this morning. She should have taken charge of the baby the instant she'd realized she likely wasn't contagious. That's why she was here. The baby was the only thing that mattered in this whole crazy mess.

The sound of gravel crunching under tires jerked her attention to the driveway. The black SUV they had arrived in slowly rolled up the drive and parked a dozen feet away. Keith sat behind the wheel.

Shana breathed a sigh of relief, but it was short-lived. Where was the baby?

She rushed to the car and flung her arms in the air, fury suddenly overtaking all other emotion. ''Where the devil have you been, Hewitt? Where's Chris?''

He glared at her as if she were in need of a straight-jacket and men in white suits. She'd considered the possibility herself already. ''What are you blabbering about?'' he demanded as he emerged from the vehicle.

Hands planted firmly on her hips, she glared right back at him. ''Where's the baby, you idiot?'' Blabbering? She didn't blabber.

Without bothering to answer, he merely opened the door to the back seat and ducked inside. Realization dawned on her then. The baby would be in the car seat right where Shana had left it when they'd arrived last night. But that still didn't tell her where he'd been and why he hadn't informed her he was leaving.

He lifted the baby, carrier and all, from the back seat and turned to her, smiling triumphantly. ''It was the only way I could get her to stop crying.''

Shana hurried to the baby, visually assuring herself that Chris was, in fact, safe and sound.

''Wait a minute.'' Keith backed away. ''You might be contagious, remember?''

Shana glowered at him. ''Don't be stupid, Hewitt. I'm fine now.'' She reached for the baby and he moved again.

"I'll take her inside. This thing is heavy."

Furious, Shana stomped after him. How dare he use her own techniques against her? And that's what he'd done. She had to give him that. He was no dummy.

Once back inside, he settled the carrier on the sofa and waited to make sure that Chris would continue sleeping. "She's fine now," he said quietly before leaving her there.

Shana noted the same and trudged after him toward the kitchen. "Where did you go?" she demanded in a harsh whisper. She wanted there to be no mistake as to the depth of her irritation.

"You cleaned up?" he commented, surprised.

"Of course I cleaned up," she snapped. "If you can cook, I can certainly clean up." Why was he avoiding her question?

"I thought you weren't feeling well," he countered, looking straight at her now, the smile he was obviously attempting to hide making one corner of his mouth twitch.

"I'm fine now," she reiterated. "Where did you go with the baby?"

He shrugged. "Nowhere. To the end of the driveway and back. She wouldn't stop crying." He shrugged again. "I'd just fed her so I knew she wasn't hungry. They do it on TV all the time."

What was he talking about? "They do what on TV?" The baby wouldn't stop crying? Why hadn't he told her?

Because she'd been playing sick.

Dread pooled in Shana's stomach, making what had felt like the right thing at the time feel all wrong.

"You know, drive kids around to get them to sleep." He grinned, a lopsided effort that diffused any hopes she'd had of staying angry with him. "It worked. She went right to sleep."

The idea that the baby had cried so much still bothered Shana. "You say you'd fed her?"

He nodded.

Puzzled, she frowned. "That doesn't make sense. Did you burp her?"

He hesitated a moment. "Certainly," he said then, clearly annoyed that she would even ask.

Chris had slept well last night. Shana had seen no indication that she suffered from colic or was one of those infants who had to be pacified at all times. Then realization dawned. "Did you change her?"

Keith didn't have to say a word. The answer was written all over his face.

"I didn't think—"

"She probably just needed a diaper change," Shana groused. "Don't you know anything?"

She said the last before she thought. The remark hit home.

"I didn't realize...." His words trailed off and a muscle pulsed in his square jaw. He was furious at her...and maybe at himself.

"We should take care of that right away," she said more calmly, contrite now. This little war of wills wasn't supposed to filter down to the baby.

"But she's asleep." The worry in his expression

told her in no uncertain terms that he feared another crying jag.

"Going too long between diaper changes can have worse consequences," Shana stated knowingly.

Deferring to her judgment, he stood by and watched as she undressed the baby. Little Chris stretched, tugging hard on Shana's heartstrings. "What a precious little girl," she cooed. "You are so darling."

Chris made sweet baby sounds, but puckered up the moment the disposable diaper was removed.

"Oh, my," Keith murmured, then cleared his throat.

"*Oh, my* is right," Shana commented dryly. The diaper was definitely in need of changing. "I think a bath is in order."

Keith blinked. "A bath?" He glanced around the room. "How do we do that?"

Shana had to smile. He was adorable when he was out of his element. "Get a couple of towels and a washcloth. The rest of what we'll need is in the diaper bag."

With the bag under her arm, she carried the baby to the kitchen sink and turned on the water. There weren't any baby bath products in the bag, but the lotion would work just fine.

Keith arrived with the requested items. "What now?" he asked as he placed them on the counter.

Shana nodded to the double sink. "Rinse this side out thoroughly and fill it with warm water."

He followed her instructions to the letter, carefully

rinsing and then filling the sink with water that was just the right temperature for the baby. Shana was impressed.

"Okay, sweetie pie," she said to the infant, "bathtime."

Chris squirmed and fretted as Shana lowered her into the water. For a moment her little face puckered up as if she might let out a howl, but she quickly settled. Those curious eyes popped open and she stared up at Shana and Keith in wonder.

"Squirt some of that—" Shana nodded to the plastic bottle on the counter "—on your hands and help me out here."

Keith frowned. "But it's lotion."

"It'll do. The soap we use would be too harsh for her skin. It'll be okay," she added when he still hesitated.

Clearly dubious, he pushed up his sleeves and squirted a generous portion in one hand, setting the bottle aside. "What now?"

"Rub it around on your palms and then reach in here and smooth it over the baby's skin."

He hesitated a second or two, then rubbed those long-fingered hands together and dipped them into the water. The baby's little head swiveled toward him as if she knew it was Keith who was attending to her now. Shana used one hand to support the little angel's head, and kept the other firmly spooned under her bottom to ensure she didn't slip. Keith tenderly caressed the baby's skin with the lotion. Before long, Shana couldn't keep her eyes off his face as he did so. The absolute fascination she saw there made her chest tighten.

With every touch, new wonder flitted across his expression. It was amazing to watch. Excited now, Baby Chris waved her arms in an effort to play. The smile her actions coaxed from that perfectly sculpted mouth of Keith Hewitt's sent Shana's heart into another of those acrobatic tumbles.

"She likes it," he whispered, as if he feared he would somehow break the spell.

"She does," Shana murmured, her gaze still glued to his amazing profile. How could any man look this sexy while bathing a baby?

"What do we do now?" He turned toward her as he spoke, his gaze colliding with hers.

Keith would have to have been blind not to recognize the way Shana was staring at him. It was like that morning when he'd almost kissed her. She looked at him as if she needed him…as if only he could give her what she ached for.

But that was impossible.

She was Shana Devlin. She hated him.

"The towel," she said, those brown eyes never leaving his. "We'll need to dry her and…"

Somehow, while he was looking at her and she was looking at him, his hand covered hers where she supported the baby's head. He hadn't meant to do it, it just happened. Her skin felt as soft as the baby's, as smooth as he'd known it would be. And over the smell of baby lotion, he could just make out her scent.

Something subtle but completely unnerving. Like the vaguest hint of roses beneath the warm sun's touch.

The baby wiggled, waving her arms frantically and jerking Keith from the trance he'd slipped into. "The towel," he muttered. He looked away and focused on the next step. The towel. Dry the baby.

"Wrap the towel around her," Shana instructed as she lifted the infant from the water.

Their hands touched again, sending a spear of heat through him, but wrapping the baby in the towel and drying her helped keep his attention focused elsewhere.

"I'll, uh, clean up," he suggested, as Shana moved back to the sofa with the baby.

Again Keith concentrated on the chore before him, or at least tried to, but Shana's singsong voice kept drawing his attention back to her. She talked that silly nonsensical talk to the baby as she dried, diapered and dressed her. Keith felt certain the sounds the baby made in response were those of happiness and contentment.

It was a good thing, he concluded. Baby Chris needed happiness right now, and Shana was more than capable of giving it to her. Maybe he'd been wrong about Shana. It could very well be that Alexandra Webber had hired Shana because she was quite talented where children were concerned.

But still... Keith turned as he dried his hands and studied the picture of woman and child. Shana Devlin was looking for something. He was certain of it. He couldn't really say he sensed deceit in her, but there was something she was after....

For just a second that morning, when she'd unbuttoned his shirt, he'd thought maybe, just maybe, she was after him, but then common sense had prevailed. Shana couldn't stand him—hated him, actually. The last thing on the planet she would want was him. She'd only agreed to come this weekend to take care of the baby.

That wasn't supposed to bother him, but somehow it did. He chastised himself for even thinking such things. This weekend was about the baby, and, for him personally, about celebrating the times he and his father had shared. He had to remember that.

But somehow Shana kept dragging him off track. Whether it was by chance or strategy, she definitely knew how to distract him.

SHANA HAD RETIRED to her room with the baby. She'd told Keith it was to ensure that Chris slept undisturbed, but that was a lie. She'd needed time away from him. Images of his face as he'd bathed the baby kept flashing through her mind. The way he'd placed his hand over hers. The way he'd looked at her.

She shivered and paced the room once more. There had to be an explanation for the way he could get to her like this. She had never been attracted to him. She was too busy despising him. Sure, she respected his work at the hospital. Everybody did. Keith Hewitt was known for championing patients' needs; that was well and good. It was his personal life she disapproved of. Her serious dislike of his carousing ways was a definite product of the way she'd been raised. She knew from personal experience how devastating a broken family could be. If a man couldn't control his baser urges while he was single, how could a woman be certain he'd behave himself once he married?

That was the big question. The one that convinced her without reservation that Keith would make a lousy husband. Even if he turned out to be a kind father, which was possible, based on what she'd witnessed in the last twelve or so hours, he couldn't be trusted otherwise. What good was a relationship without trust?

Relationship? Why on earth was she worrying about relationships and Keith Hewitt at the same time? What he did and with whom he did it was none of her concern. She'd simply made a decision to upset his ego during their forced proximity. That's all.

She stopped midstep. Was that really all? She swallowed nervously. Surely she wasn't falling victim to his charms? Shana hugged her arms around herself. Wouldn't she know it if what she'd planned was some sort of subconscious scheme to get closer to him?

Shaking her head, she stormed over to the French doors and swung them wide. That was insane. No way would she stoop to such a level. She didn't need sex that badly. She stepped out into the crisp afternoon air. Sure, it had been a while. A while, hell. It had been two years.

A heavy sigh slipped past her lips as she closed her

eyes and forced away the thought. What did it matter
how long it had been? Sex wasn't for sport. It was a
shared intimacy between two people who really cared
about each other, wanted a future together. To her
way of thinking, that kind of intimacy didn't come
along every week or even every month. She glared
out at the trees swaying gently in the breeze. Unlike
some people, she considered sharing her body with a
man to be a kind of sacred thing, something done only
when two people reached a very important stage in a
relationship. It was about forever.

That thinking was old-fashioned, she knew, but it
was the way she felt. Guys like Keith Hewitt would
consider her prudish or even frigid. He had no concept whatsoever of that kind of commitment. She definitely intended to keep a wide berth emotionally
where he was concerned. He'd already managed to
make her rethink some of her previous notions about
him. But as her mother had often said, actions spoke
louder than words. Just because he seemed sincere
and caring where the baby was concerned didn't mean
he really was.

She couldn't recall once hearing anyone talk about
his family or his visits with them. What kind of man
stayed away from his family, avoided talking about
them? She'd seen the pictures on the mantel downstairs. Maybe there had been some kind of falling out
between him and his father. And what about his
mother? She hadn't seen a photograph of his mom.
She supposed his parents could be deceased, but she'd
never heard anything to indicate he was all alone in

the world. Admittedly, though, unlike his social life, Keith kept his personal life to himself. Surely he had a mother or father somewhere.

The ability to cut off all ties with family spoke loudly and clearly of one thing: a lack of basic human compassion. Keith had to be truly coldhearted to turn off his emotions so easily. No matter what she thought she saw in him when he held the baby, it could all be for show.

She'd seen the hunger in his eyes. He wanted her. Truth be told, she appeared to be suffering from the same ailment. But unlike her unexpected attraction, his was probably calculated. No doubt hers was merely a result of having gone too long without physical contact with a man.

Shana exhaled another heavy breath. Enough on that subject. She didn't want to think about sex and Keith Hewitt anymore. In fact, she didn't want to think about him at all until this was over and there was some distance between them. He had apparently honed his skills of seduction to the point where he could easily sway even his staunchest adversary. Well, she had no intention of ending up one of his conquests.

Not now, not ever.

Just then his broad shoulders and equally amazing backside came into view. To her supreme annoyance, her breath caught. Before she could properly curse her vulnerability, she noted two things. He was heading into the woods, and he carried a fishing pole. One very much like the pole he'd had in the picture with his father. He was also dressed in similar jeans, flannel shirt and waders. The only thing missing from the picture was his father.

Just what was the deal, she wondered again, with Keith and his family?

Had he done something so terrible that they no longer wanted anything to do with him? She doubted that. Mothers and fathers usually loved their children no matter what they did. It was part of being a parent—unconditional love.

The thought drew her back into the room and to the bed where Baby Chris slept.

Who would love this baby that way? Who would care for her? Fix her lunch and send her off to school when the time came? Or dress her up for the prom and teach her how to walk in her first set of high-heeled shoes?

Who would kiss her cheek at night and smile down at her no matter what harsh words they'd shared earlier that evening, or what transgression the teenager she would become had managed?

The answer was a mystery…just like Baby Chris's true identity.

Tears welled unbidden in Shana's eyes. Somehow she had to see that someone, somewhere, did all those things for this child. No baby should be without the love and support of good parents. As bumpy as her own childhood had been at times, Shana had never once doubted that she was loved immensely. Her mother had always been there when Shana needed her. When her first crush on a boy broke her heart at the tender age of thirteen. When her best friend moved away. When the man she'd loved like a father disappeared from her life.

Every child deserved at least one loving parent.

And one way or another, Baby Chris would have one.

CHAPTER SIX

THE SMELL OF SOMETHING delectable lured Shana from her nap. She sighed, feeling rested. Then the memory of all that had happened in the last twenty-four hours slammed into her.

She was in a cabin in the woods with Keith Hewitt...alone.

Except for the baby.

Shana lifted her head and peered at the clock, then smiled down at Baby Chris, who lay snuggled against her breasts. A feeling of completeness sifted through her. This was what motherhood was like—this sensation of happiness that bloomed deep in her chest.

She hoped that someday she would find this kind of happiness and completeness with a husband and child—or children—of her own.

Abruptly, and to her utter chagrin, the image of Keith Hewitt blossomed in her mind.

"Not in this lifetime," she muttered as she cautiously climbed from the bed without disturbing little Chrissy. Shana stretched languidly. Goodness, she'd only meant to lie down with the baby long enough to get her to sleep.

Her stomach rumbled as she once again inhaled the

delicious fragrance drifting up from the kitchen. Keith might not be husband material, but apparently he was one hell of a good cook. She could scarcely believe she'd slept until 7:00 p.m. Eating would be really good about now.

Shana quickly placed the bureau-drawer-turned-cradle in the center of the bed and tucked a sleeping Chris safely inside on the fluffy blanket. Ensuring that the bedroom door was left wide-open so that the baby's cries could be heard, she hurried downstairs to find out what was on tonight's menu.

At the bottom of the stairs she stopped, unable to take another step, her gaze riveted on the man in the kitchen. A dish towel was slung carelessly over his left shoulder. He was lifting what looked and smelled like seared fish filets from a sizzling pan and placing them neatly on a white stoneware platter. As she watched, the oven dinged and he turned efficiently in that direction and removed a tray of biscuits.

This was too much. He couldn't possibly have made those from scratch, and she hadn't noticed any of the canned, refrigerated variety. She scanned the countertop for telltale signs of flour and leftover dough, but found none. She'd seen the kind of mess he left when he cooked, though she supposed he could have cleaned up after himself this time. Setting the biscuits aside, he deftly stirred something in a pot on the stovetop.

Before she could stop herself, she sank down on the steps to observe him as he worked. Unaware of her presence, he went about his business totally off guard. She couldn't remember ever seeing him appear this relaxed. If she'd thought that face handsome under normal conditions, the man was absolutely devastating when thoroughly at ease. Those angles and edges were just a tad softer, more forgiving. The lines of impatience that generally marred his brow were missing now. He looked young…and vulnerable.

The transformation was incredible. Who was this man? she wondered, mesmerized. Those long-fingered hands moved with grace and confidence as he mounded those luscious biscuits on the platter with the mouthwatering filets. With the platter centered on the island, he transferred the contents of the pot— green beans and small potatoes—into a glass bowl and settled it next to the platter. He stood back and regarded his work for a moment. Apparently satisfied, he dried his hands with the towel and tossed it next to the sink.

As if he'd suddenly sensed her presence, his gaze leaped to hers, and Shana's cheeks flushed. Heat, the same intensity that colored her cheeks but of a different nature, seared straight through her middle. For one long moment they simply stared at each other, then those impatient lines furrowed his brow, banishing all signs of vulnerability.

"I was just about to come up and let you know dinner was ready," he said suspiciously.

Rising slowly to her feet, Shana replied, "No need. The heavenly smells called me first."

He looked away, evidently not thrilled that she'd been watching him. "Let's not let it get cold."

Again, the question of who Keith Hewitt really was filtered through her mind. But did she want to know? Did it matter in the grand scheme of things? Maybe. Probably not.

Shana joined him in the kitchen and took two glasses from the cabinet, where she'd found them earlier that day. "What would you like to drink?"

Keith deposited two plates on the counter and considered her question. "There's white wine. Or beer if you'd prefer."

Beer sounded good to her. She replaced the glasses where she'd found them and stuck her head in the fridge. Sure enough, there was beer way in the back. She hadn't even noticed it when she'd gotten out orange juice to wash down those pancakes. Quickly she scanned for ready-made biscuits. *Nada.*

But that didn't mean they hadn't been there. A quick peek in the freezer compartment revealed his secret. A clear plastic bag of small round cakes of frozen biscuit dough sat in plain view. Well, she allowed, they might not be homemade, but she'd had that kind before and they were delicious.

With two long-neck bottles of beer waiting on the table alongside paper napkins and plain flatware, she and Keith loaded their plates, trying hard not to bump each other. The great room seemed too small for the two of them. The kitchen definitely shrank in his presence.

Too famished to dwell on the definite sparks flying, Shana hurried to the table and slid onto one of the ladder-back chairs. She couldn't wait to bite into that fish. It smelled so good.

She moaned with satisfaction when she did. It was absolutely delicious.

"What did you do to this stuff? It's great." The words were scarcely out of her mouth before she shoveled in another bite.

Keith looked entirely too smug, but the cuisine was so good she forgave him readily.

"Caught 'em, cleaned 'em and fried 'em up," he retorted.

The memory of him tramping off into the woods, fishing pole in hand, zoomed through her mind's eye. She stared down at the filet she'd more than half consumed, then up at the man across the table. Despite the pictures on the mantel, the reality that he'd actually caught these fish with his own two hands and prepared them for their dinner amazed her.

"How?" She shook her head. "I mean, do you do this often?" Did he spend every weekend here? Was that why the place was so well stocked?

"The usual way," he said, his tone teasing. "With a hook and line." He placed a forkful of the tender white meat into that sensual mouth and chewed slowly, as if savoring each distinct flavor and texture. "And yes," he added after he'd swallowed. "I come here when I can."

"You keep everything stocked like this all the time?" She was digging, but she just couldn't help herself. She wanted to know this side of him, maybe to convince herself it was real.

A wall went up; she saw it as clearly as if it had been made of bricks. "At times. Usually on holiday weekends."

There it was. Shana sipped her beer, enjoyed the taste and feel of the cool, bubbly liquid as it slid down her throat. He spent all his holiday weekends here. Away from his family. All alone. Before her obviously skewed imagination could take over completely, she reminded herself that he probably never spent a night alone. And there was the photo with his father.

"I suppose your girlfriends like the cozy cabin and the solitude," she said, going for flippant but failing miserably. It came out more like jealousy. What she'd meant was that his female conquests probably enjoyed his full attention...for as long as it lasted, anyway.

Confusion joined the impatience and annoyance she usually saw on his face. "I always come here alone."

She hadn't meant to laugh; it had just popped out. Shana covered her mouth with her hand. "Sorry." Her cheeks burned again.

A glower replaced the confusion. "I don't think you are." He took a long drink from his own beer and plopped the bottle back onto the table. "You really believe that all I do—" he flung his arms upward in something resembling frustration "—is run after women." He shot a pointed look at her. "You know, my love life is none of your business. But just so you know, I'm quite selective about whom I socialize with, present company notwithstanding.''

This time she laughed outright, even if he had insulted her. ''Get real, Hewitt. Everyone at the hospital knows your reputation. You've dated most of the female staff under forty. The women get together and vote you most eligible bachelor every year.'' She leaned forward slightly and adopted an I-know-what-I'm-talking-about tone. ''Actions speak louder than words.''

''You really believe all that gossip?''

Something about the way he asked the question disarmed her. She'd been ready to refute anything he said, but the question he asked was definitely not what she'd been expecting.

She shrugged. ''The way I hear it, it isn't gossip.''

He shook his head and turned back to his food. ''Believe what you will.''

Talk about letdowns. His resigned statement pulled the plug on Shana's battle preparations. She'd been ready for a fight, the usual sparring. Now all that adrenaline was swirling around the proverbial drain. No point letting it go to waste.

''You're saying it's not true,'' she prodded, hoping to yank him back into fighting mode, or at least to counter the sinking feeling in the pit of her stomach.

That fierce amber gaze met hers. ''I'm saying don't believe everything you hear. What I do at the hospital is about work. Taking care of the patients…'' He shook his head and refused to say more.

She waved her hand in a chopping motion. ''Wait

just one minute. You're not getting off that easily. How do you equate flirting and womanizing with patient care?"

He stared at her for a long moment, as if weighing her worthiness to hear what he had to say.

"I want to know the truth," she added for good measure.

KEITH PUSHED AWAY his plate. She wanted to know the truth, did she? People never really wanted to know the truth. They wanted to have their presumption of truth confirmed.

"The truth." He tossed his wadded paper napkin onto the table. "It's my motto that if you give people what they want, you get what you want in return."

He had to smile at her appalled expression. As usual, she'd totally misconstrued his words. But that didn't stop him from saying the rest. "In my experience, it's worth the trouble to see that my patients and their families get the best care possible."

"And you accomplish this by bedding the female staff?"

Now, that annoyed him. Why did people always jump to the worst conclusions? "Check your sources, Ms. Devlin. You'll find that I've 'bedded,' as you so eloquently put it, far fewer women than you apparently believe."

"Wait a minute."

There she went, waving those arms again. The woman had to be the most demonstrative human being he'd ever met. He suddenly wondered if she'd be as animated in bed. Forcing the idea away, he focused on her next accusation.

"You're telling me that you haven't slept with—"

Before she could start naming names, he simply shook his head. The truth was, he hadn't slept with any of the women at the hospital, but he wasn't going to tell Shana that. It was none of her business. He'd made it a rule when he came to work there: socializing was okay, but no intimate relationships. He flirted, yes. He teased. He always tried to be friendly and affable to help keep everyone happy and cooperative, but nothing more. He sought physical intimacy elsewhere. Seattle was a large city. Finding single, willing females wasn't a problem.

"But I've heard the things they say," she insisted, determined to defend her stand. "Things like how amazing you are, and that you're a god between the sheets." She snapped her mouth shut, her cheeks flaming beautifully once more.

Keith couldn't help smiling at her embarrassment. She had no one to blame but herself. "Maybe they do think I'm amazing." He grinned sheepishly. "The god thing might be a bit of a stretch, but—" he looked squarely into those wide, expressive eyes, unshielded now without the glasses she sometimes wore at work "—I can assure you those remarks were not based on personal experience."

Shana fiddled with her napkin, turning it end over end. "Of course you'd deny it. Men like you—"

"Men like me…?" he inquired as he propped his elbow on the table and rested his chin in his hand.

He couldn't help thoroughly enjoying her discomfort. He should let her off the hook and just agree with whatever she said. It would be the simplest thing to do. The safest as well. Allowing the females at the hospital to believe what they would had protected his single status thus far. What was it about this woman that made him want to come clean?

Maybe it was those touch-me auburn locks that hugged her face and just begged to be caressed. Or that incredible vulnerability in those big brown eyes. No, no, it had to be that perfect, lush mouth. Even now, when she was so unsettled, he could imagine those lips on his. On his skin...

He blinked the fantasy away. *Focus, man,* he warned himself silently.

"You know," she was saying. "Men who consider women just playthings." She squared those slender shoulders and leveled her gaze on him. "Men who can't be counted on, who don't know how to commit for the long haul. Men who walk away without looking back."

The pain that welled in her eyes told him she was speaking from personal experience. Someone had hurt her badly.

"As long as we're playing truth or dare," he offered, relaxing in his seat, "you might as well take your turn."

She blinked those long lashes to hide her surprise, or perhaps the fear his question elicited.

He raised an inquiring eyebrow. "You're not one of those people who want to know all about everyone else but who refuse to divulge their own secrets, are you?''

"I…there's nothing to tell." She pushed back her chair and stood abruptly. "I'll clean up if you'll check on the baby."

Now who was playing duck and dodge?

"Sure," he said placatingly. "I'll check on the baby and then I'll be back to help you clean up." He stood and pushed his chair into place. "Then you can tell me all about Shana Devlin."

SHANA STOOD FROZEN in place as he bounded up the stairs. How in the world had she let the discussion escalate into this? She didn't want him knowing anything about her. Her heart stumbled once, twice, before it kicked back into an acceptable rhythm. If she let this get personal, he would weasel his way into her heart and then he'd break it. The way the good-looking ones always did. What had happened to her plan? All hopes of teaching him a lesson evaporated whenever he was near.

No matter what he said, she was still convinced he was a commitment avoider and a womanizer of the worst kind. He was blatant about it and unapologetic. Sure, he might be extra friendly to everyone to see that he got what he wanted, and the patients might just benefit in the long run, but the end did not always justify the means.

She heard his footfalls on the upstairs landing once more. She had to have a plan. Snatching up their plates and rushing to the sink, she thought frantically about how she would counter his assault. She needed a strategy....

"Okay," he said as he came up behind her. "Where were we?"

She emptied the remainders of their meal into the trash and loaded the plates into the dishwasher. "You had decided we were going to play truth or dare." She said this without looking at him. She couldn't risk exposing her emotions right now. He evidently read her quite easily.

"So, Shana, tell me some truth about you," he said casually.

While she groped for something to say, he gathered the beer bottles from the table and tossed them into the recycling bin. As if it was second nature, he reached for a dishcloth and began wiping down the table and countertops.

The way he appeared so at home in the kitchen still unbalanced her. It was totally unexpected, like his assertion that he hadn't slept with all those women at the hospital.

"I don't trust you." Her words echoed in the room, and for two eternal seconds she couldn't believe she'd said them. What was she thinking?

His head came up and he looked at her as if he couldn't believe it, either.

The silence stretched for a full ten seconds.

"In what way don't you trust me?"

Well, she'd opened up that can of worms, so she might as well fish. "You're too smooth, too charming...." She shrugged. "Too good-looking. Men like you are hard to trust."

The grin that affected only one side of his mouth made another appearance. "You think I'm good-looking? And charming?"

God, why didn't the floor just split open and swallow her up? "Well...yes." No point in lying. The guy wasn't blind. He had to know he was handsome.

He straightened from the countertop and moved in her direction. Each step was so deliberate, so measured that she found herself holding her breath. He tossed the cloth into the sink and stared down at her, where she remained paralyzed near the dishwasher.

"If it makes you feel any better, I think you're very attractive, as well." He leaned one hip against the sink. "But I don't trust you, either."

A kind of shock quaked through her, whether from his proximity or his admission, she couldn't say. "What does that mean?" she snapped, once again allowing her emotions to show. Damn it. She didn't like the way he could draw out her reactions so easily. And why didn't he trust her? That was ridiculous.

"What brought you to Seattle? What're you running away from?"

She stiffened, this time with fury. She wasn't running from anything. How dare he even suggest it? "I'm not running." She spat the words at him. She absolutely would not dignify that question by discussing it further. "Besides, you've already had your question. It's my turn."

He splayed those wide, oh-so-masculine hands. "Shoot."

She folded her arms over her chest. "If what you say is true, that you spend holidays here alone, tell me why you don't share them with family? You do have family, don't you?"

This time he was the one who tensed. Gone was that smug expression. He didn't like being asked really personal questions. Well, he was the one who'd started this.

"I don't have any family," he said flatly. "I was an only child and my mother died when I was just a kid. My father passed away last year from a heart attack."

Talk about feeling like the scum of the earth. Shana was speechless. What could she say to that? *I'm sorry?* That was too lame. But the hurt in his eyes— in his very posture—told her how much that admission had cost him.

"I'm sorry," she murmured lamely. "I just thought…" She glanced across the room at the mantel. "I saw the pictures and I thought…"

He followed her gaze. "That was our last fishing trip together. Columbus Day weekend last year. It was the last time I saw him alive."

God, she was such a heel. "That's why you were so determined to come here this weekend?" she asked gently.

He continued to stare in the direction of the photos for a moment before he turned back to her. "Yes. Only one other person knows that. Jaron."

She licked her lips and went for a change of subject. "I didn't know you and Detective Dorsey were such good friends."

That amber gaze bored into hers with such ferocity that she had to physically restrain the urge to flinch. "There are a lot of things you don't know about me."

"Well, there are things you don't know about me, either. Besides…besides Alexandra," she stuttered, searching for a way to set the conversation to rights, "Annabelle Peters is a good friend of mine." Shana gestured vaguely, uncertain what to do with her hands. "We live right next to each other. She's got this big old dog named Harold. I walk him for her sometimes. We kind of help each other out."

Keith only nodded.

She hugged her arms around herself once more and dredged up a smile. "So, who takes care of this place for you?" She glanced around. She'd told him something more about herself, and now it was his turn. "It's so nice. Surely you don't have time to see after everything yourself."

He blinked, as if he were coming out of some sort of trance. "There's a fellow who lives on the other side of the creek who takes care of some of the vacation cabins. He's very reliable. He always stocks the kitchen for me when I let him know I'm coming." Keith glanced around, as if seeing the cabin for the first time. "I wasn't able to get up here all summer." A frown lined his brow. "Memorial Day weekend was the last time this year, I think."

"It's really nice," she said, although she was pretty

sure she'd already said that once. "Really nice. I've never been much of an outdoorsy person. That's my brother's forte, not mine."

Keith's frown deepened. "You have a brother?"

She nodded. "Brett is back home in Nebraska. Refuses to get to know Alexandra." She sighed, wondering why in the world she was telling Keith all this. "I miss him."

"No other family?"

The intensity in his voice made her shiver. Was he closer now, or was that just her imagination? She resisted the urge to ease back a step. She wasn't afraid of Keith Hewitt. He didn't have her fooled...not really.

She shook her head, then remembered her stepfather. "Well, there's my stepfather. Alexandra's father. He practically raised me and Brett." A genuine smile claimed her lips as she thought of the sweet man who'd taken up the slack in their fatherless home. She'd been so hurt when he went away, but now she knew he hadn't done so on purpose, and that made things much better.

Keith nodded. "That's why you came to Seattle?"

Her gaze bumped into his, and there was no way to miss the desire shining in those eyes. She swallowed tightly and urged her heart to slow. She wasn't supposed to react to him, wasn't going to be swayed by his charms. It would be a huge mistake.

"Partly," she confessed, and then could have bitten off her tongue. Why was she admitting anything to him? She shouldn't even be here. She should be upstairs with the baby, far away from those hypnotic eyes....

"There's another reason?"

He was definitely closer now. She could feel the warmth of his breath on her lips. Her pulse was racing; something hot and wild sang in her veins. Oh, God, she wanted him to kiss her. It was true. No matter how much she tried to deny it, it was true!

"Yes," she whispered.

"You could..." His gaze was on her mouth, his attention apparently splintered, since he fell silent.

He licked those lips and reason fled. She couldn't take any more of this. Shana flung her arms around his neck and kissed him. He froze, but she just kept on kissing him. What the hell? Get it over with. And then his arms were around her, hauling her up against his hard, lean body. He kissed her back and she all but melted against him. His lips were firm but soft somehow...his body was like molten steel, and hers molded to every male contour. He tasted like beer and spices and red-hot male.

Whatever she'd believed about Keith Hewitt— whatever she'd wanted to deny, to refute—she could say one thing with absolute certainty now. The man knew how to kiss a woman.

CHAPTER SEVEN

KEITH SURRENDERED to the kiss, to the sweet taste of Shana and the temptation she offered. Those firm, voluptuous breasts pressed against his chest. She felt so good in his arms. Felt right.

He tensed.

What the hell was he thinking?

He drew away from that lush, hungry mouth and stared down at the soft, pliant woman in his arms. Those big brown eyes were dazed, those succulent lips slightly parted. Her breath came in rapid little puffs.

He'd kissed Shana Devlin.

Dear God.

It was true.

He had gone mad.

No…wait.

She'd kissed him.

A frown creased his brow and he promptly set the startled woman away from him. "Why did you do that?" he demanded sharply.

All that soft vulnerability instantly morphed into female fury. "You kissed me!" she accused, her entire body rigid with anger.

He blinked, startled by the intensity of her reaction. "But…you kissed me first. I was only responding to what you initiated."

She shook her head, flustered. "That's…that's…" She looked at him then, confusion filling those wide, expressive eyes. "Oh Lord…you're right," she admitted. "I'm sorry." She backed up a step and crossed her arms over her breasts in a protective manner, hiding from view those pert nipples that showed through her blouse, begging for attention. He blinked again. He had to get back on track here.

"I don't know what got into me." She shook her head again. "This was a mistake."

Her gaze locked with his and the trepidation and uncertainty he saw there tied his gut in knots.

"I shouldn't have come, but—" she looked toward the upstairs landing "—the baby…"

"It's all right." Keith stepped toward Shana, causing her to retreat a step. "It was as much my fault as yours," he reasoned defeatedly. He shrugged. "We both got a little carried away."

She nodded, still looking far too uncertain of him as well as herself.

"We should start over." He exhaled a heavy breath. "Try to be friends." He glanced toward the stairs to emphasize his point. "The baby will pick up on our tension. She needs positive reassurance right now."

Shana followed his gaze. "You're right."

"Another beer?" They definitely needed a break from the tension. Relax, have a beer, talk a little…

The memory of that kiss replayed in his head, hardening muscles in his body that were already far too inflexible for comfort.

She managed a strained smile. "That'd be great."

Only then did he notice how red and kiss-swollen her lips were. Guilt swamped him. Yes, she'd started it, but he'd finished it in a very big way.

Grabbing two bottles of beer en route, Keith followed Shana to the sofa. He handed her one and opted to take the chair across from her to allow some semblance of personal space.

"You and Annabelle are friends?" he asked, kicking off what he hoped would be a much more relaxed conversation.

She sipped her beer and looked anywhere but at him. "That's right. We kind of fell into the relationship. It wasn't intentional. She needed help with her dog and I was more than happy to oblige." Her gaze finally returned to his. "What about you and Detective Dorsey?"

"I knew Jaron before...before he lost his wife." Keith hated recalling that day, almost as much as he hated looking back on the day his own mother had died. "But only in passing. I'd seen him around." He took a long draw from his beer. "But that night in the E.R. when...she died...well, it changed things for Jaron and his kids and was similar to the way my own life had changed a long time ago. I guess we connected because of that mutual experience. We've been good friends ever since."

Shana studied him for a long while, and he was

certain he'd said too much. He hadn't meant to, hadn't intended to mention himself in the explanation.

"You lost someone?" She blinked. "I mean, a girlfriend or...wife?"

She said the last as if the idea were unthinkable. How had she convinced herself that he wasn't capable of deeper feelings when she didn't even know him? The idea that she might be right gave him pause.

Realization settled in his stomach like a rock. She'd come to that conclusion because he'd wanted it that way...had ensured that no one got close. No one except Jaron, and even he only knew what Keith wanted him to know. It was easier that way. If you steered clear of that level of commitment, then you weren't likely to lose anything that mattered that much.

"No...it was my mother," he admitted, knowing Shana wouldn't drop the topic until he explained. "I was only eight and it was pretty frightening for a boy all alone."

A frown lined her smooth brow. "But what about your father?" She curled her legs up on the sofa and relaxed against the arm. Aged leather squeaked beneath her slight weight as she shifted.

She looked at home...at home on his sofa. The idea made him uneasy, restless somehow, but he pushed it away. They were supposed to be getting comfortable. That's what this little talk was all about.

"My father was in the military. Special Forces," he explained when she still looked confused. "Sometimes he would be gone for months and we wouldn't know where he was. It was a military secret." Keith stared at the bottle in his hands. "It took a while for our dependent sponsor to track him down."

He didn't look at her. Didn't want to see the sympathy in her eyes. He'd seen far too much of that all those years ago.

"Surely there was someone—some aunt or uncle or cousin who took care of you while—"

"There was no one," he said, cutting her off. Memories he'd just as soon forget made his voice grim. "I got bounced from foster home to foster home for months. There weren't enough places to go around, and no one wanted to keep a rambunctious, unhappy little boy for longer than a week or two."

Shana swallowed back the emotion that welled in her throat as she listened. He'd been left all alone…completely alone…with strangers. Was this what made him careful about not getting deeply involved with anyone? Was this the reason he flitted from woman to woman, avoiding commitment?

"That's—" she shook her head when the words to describe the tragedy weren't forthcoming "—awful," she finally said for lack of a more appropriate adjective. "That time had to be immensely difficult for you." She looked at him then. For just one second she saw the scared little boy from the past lurking in those amber eyes, then the emotion vanished so quickly she wondered if she'd really seen it at all.

"I got over it." He leaned forward and propped his elbows on his spread knees, dangling the bottle of beer from the fingertips of one hand.

Watching him now and thinking about all that she

knew, Shana wondered if he had really gotten over it. She, of all people, knew that the past—good, bad or indifferent—colored a person's present and future with a broad stroke. Fight though she might, she could never outrun the lessons she'd learned growing up. The loss of her father, the hurt she'd watched her mother staunchly pretend wasn't real, had had a strong impact. Then the stepfather she'd loved had left them, as well. And though Shana now knew that her mother had brought some of what had happened on herself, the unhappy events had made quite an impression. Everyone learned from their life situation. Keith Hewitt would be no different.

He could struggle to overcome the experience, to leave it behind, but those old hurts influenced everything he said and did. Maybe he was right on that one score: maybe she'd judged him wrongly simply because he was too good-looking for her comfort.

"Do we ever really get over the past?" she heard herself say. She didn't expect an answer, it was more a rhetorical question.

"We do what we do," he said tightly. "Blaming the past is the easy way out. That's the trouble with people nowadays." His tone grew harsher with each uttered word. "No one wants to take responsibility for their actions. They blame the past or their parents or both."

Shana recoiled emotionally from his savage response. Boy, was he in denial. "Maybe you're right, but don't you think that Baby Chris's life has been irrevocably altered in a way that she might someday be resentful of? Everything was taken away from her in one fatal instant. Who will she blame? The truck driver? Her father's lack of attention while driving? Fate? God?''

The look Keith directed at her made Shana shiver. She'd hit a nerve again.

''Why blame anyone? Why not just get over it and make the best of your life?''

''Like you did?'' The moment the words were out of her mouth she knew she'd made a mistake. White-hot fury washed over his face, stiffened his posture.

''I knew admitting anything to you would be a mistake. Why would you face life when you can run away from it?''

That same fury she'd seen overtake him flooded her now. ''I told you, I'm not running from anything or anyone,'' she countered icily. He was like a dog with a bone. ''For your information, I came to Seattle because I wanted to. Because I wanted to embrace *more* of my past.'' *It's my brother who wants to hide from it,* she could have added.

Keith looked far from swayed. ''What about your lifelong friends? The rest of your family? Surely there were cousins, aunts, uncles, besides your brother. You simply walked away from all of it and came here to a stranger.''

Just what was he accusing her of? ''People move all the time—leave distant relatives, even close ones, behind. You think I don't know how to use a phone or pick up a pen and paper? I keep in touch.''

''But you're not going back, right?''

The question sent a rush of cold through her. Was she going back? She hadn't really thought about it. What was back there? She didn't have any other family, as he'd suggested, except for Brett. Sure, she had friends, but what with college and her mother's illness, they'd lost touch after high school. And certainly there was no waiting boyfriend.

"That's what I thought," Keith said knowingly. Too knowingly.

"What's wrong with starting a new life?" she demanded, taken aback by his accusatory tone. People did it all the time after college. She had a right to begin her career in a new town far away from home. So what if she was getting a late start? Taking care of her mother had come first.

A twinge of homesickness pinched her. She blinked back the emotion that accompanied it. That he could see right through her made her want to slap his smug face.

"What about you?" she demanded. "The way I hear it, you came to Seattle Memorial just three years ago. Where was home for you before that?"

He smiled even more smugly. "You get no points there. I left nearby Tacoma General only because Seattle Memorial was in such dire need of a social services director."

Shana rolled her eyes and took another sip of her beer. Damn him. He had an answer for everything. Mr. Keith Hewitt the perfect never made a mistake.

A pang of guilt struck her when she thought of the frightened little boy he'd been. But that was a long time ago, she reminded her softer side. That frightened little boy had turned into a hard-edged, emotionless man.

Yet another little voice mocked her. *And what about that kiss?* it taunted. There had been some definite emotion and fire in that kiss. She couldn't deny it.

So they were sexually attracted. Even criminals had sexual urges. The fact that chemistry stirred between them didn't make them compatible.

She resisted the urge to smack herself on the forehead with the heel of her hand. Why was this monologue running in her head? She didn't want to be attracted to him. She didn't want to be compatible on any level. And she definitely didn't want a relationship with a good-looking, womanizing guy—no matter how caring he was about his work. Enough said.

"You know," she said, pushing herself to her feet, "that fish was really good. Maybe I'll have seconds." She was stuffed now, but she needed a distraction. Since there was no television, food would have to do. Feigning hunger, she delved in the fridge for the leftovers.

"Fresh fish is always the best," he said from the other side of the open fridge door.

She jerked upright, almost hitting her head on the freezer compartment. He'd followed her! He had no intention of letting this thing go.

"You want some, too?" she asked, waving the covered platter in front of him.

He lifted one shoulder in an indifferent shrug. "Why not?"

"My brother used to bring home his catch of the day from time to time." She rambled as she retrieved a couple of plates and divvied up the leftovers. "He always tried to talk me into going fishing with him, but I never would." She shuddered at the thought. "No way."

"You've never been fishing?"

At his shocked tone, she glanced up. He looked downright flabbergasted. "No. Why? Is that some sort of unforgivable sin?" The words came out a little more acerbic than she'd intended. Why was it she couldn't hide her true feelings from this man?

He laughed...sort of. The sound was a little choked. "Everyone should go fishing at least once. It could save your life."

She arched an eyebrow skeptically. "If I were lost in the woods near water?"

He growled, "No. It's a great way to relieve stress. You just sit out there in the peace and quiet and relax with nothing but you and the wide-open spaces." He sighed wistfully. "The sound of the water lapping against the shore...the breeze..."

She was shaking her head before he finished presenting his case. "Yeah, yeah, yeah, I get it, but no thanks. There'll be bugs and snakes." She shook her head more resolutely now. "No way. I told you before, I'm not the outdoorsy type."

"We'll use bug repellent," he insisted. "Really, there won't be that many bugs out this late in the year, especially if we go early." He inclined that handsome head to one side. "Snakes aren't that big a concern, either. The creek where I fish is perfectly safe."

Trepidation climbed up her spine. "The morning air will probably be too cool for Chris," she argued. A bad feeling crept over her. She wasn't going to win this debate.

"The weather report for tomorrow is good. Trust me, the baby will enjoy the outing as well," he said succinctly, as if he had a crystal ball and could see the future and knew just how the day would turn out.

This would be another mistake. Maybe not as monumental as the kiss had been, but a mistake all the same. "I don't think that's a good idea. Besides, Chris is a baby—she won't remember anything about it."

"The fresh air and silence will be good for her," he countered, unwilling to relent. "The quiet time and stress relief will be good for you...and me." That slumberous, lionlike gaze captured hers once more. "We need a break from the confines of this cabin."

He was right about that much. The coming night— with him in the next room, was not going to be conducive to sleep. Especially knowing how much she wanted him on a physical level... God, how she hated to admit that. And judging by that kiss, he wasn't unaffected himself. They needed a time-out, a distraction.

Fishing.

What the heck.

She might even enjoy it.

CHAPTER EIGHT

WELL, HE'D BEEN RIGHT about one thing; there were hardly any bugs.

But he'd failed to mention the occasional briar, and the lack of a place to sit other than on the ground.

And the worms.

He bragged that he'd dug them himself.

Slimy, wriggling little creatures that he slid onto a hook. If they were lucky, they died instantly.

Shana wanted to gag.

"See? This is great." He beamed as he cast her line into the water and offered her the pole. "Now, just sit back and enjoy the peace and quiet."

Yeah, right. Giving the thing a cool once-over, she accepted it. Keith Hewitt didn't use fancy reels and rods. No, he did this the old-fashioned way. Yuck.

She held the pole gingerly, not even pretending to like it. She leaned to the right and checked on little Chris once more. Still sleeping peacefully. The baby had fretted a bit on the trip through the woods, but Shana was pretty sure that was because she didn't like the car seat. Once Shana had lifted the baby in her arms and left Keith with the seat and fishing gear to haul, all had been well.

Chris simply liked being close to a warm body, and Shana couldn't blame her for that.

Immediately an image of her warm, naked body aligned perfectly with Keith's filled the private theater of her mind. She blinked the forbidden fantasy away and stared at the rustic fishing implement in her hands. She refused to think about the man. Though she'd learned a few things that lessened her animosity toward him just a teensy bit, he was still the enemy. The kind of man who could break her heart.

She'd protected her heart pretty darn well up to this point. Why fall down on the job now?

She shot him a sidelong glance. Not even a guy as good-looking as Keith was worth the risk. She turned away from that sexy profile and stared out over the creek. Nope, he wasn't worth it.

KEITH STRUGGLED TO KEEP his full attention on the two red-and-white floaters riding the surface of the still water. But it proved damn difficult.

All night long he'd lain in his bed and thought about the woman down the hall. He'd battled the images his mind had played over and over, but he'd lost miserably. Nothing he'd done had blocked out thoughts of how she looked, smelled and tasted. If he hadn't lost himself to that kiss… If he'd left well enough alone and never allowed himself to know just how sweetly delicious she was…

It was too late for ifs now. He'd had that taste. And like Adam and that confounded apple, he was doomed.

Doomed to the next forty-eight hours in pure hell.
He could think of nothing else—dream of nothing
else—but making love to her in a dozen long, slow
ways.

He closed his eyes and tamped down the urge to
reach out and touch her. Damn it, how could he want
her this much? They didn't even like each other. A
little sigh hissed past his lips and he forced his eyes
open.

That talk last night had relieved him of a few of
his former notions. There appeared to be more to
Shana Devlin than he'd first suspected. Maybe she
wasn't just a pretty piece of fluff floating about, taking what she could here and there. He'd watched her
with the baby…had almost lost his mind during that
bath. Merely touching her hand had aroused him.
Tasting her lips had tipped him over the edge. No
kiss had ever blown him away as that one had.

He'd always been in control.

Always.

He never allowed his emotions to rule him. How
in hell had this happened? He couldn't keep his head
on straight for more than five minutes in her presence.
Just watching her move, listening to her voice, drove
him crazy. Made him want to touch her everywhere
at once.

His fingers tightened on the fishing pole. It could
be nothing more than the worn-out adage that opposites attract. Maybe it was just the need to have what
was out of his reach. His gut tightened at the thought
of having her.

He had a very bad feeling that it was far more than that. Somehow, some way, he had a thing for Shana. He couldn't define *what,* but it was there. And it was bursting at the seams to get out. If he wasn't careful... He didn't even want to think what could happen.

Shifting his gaze to the baby, he told himself again that this weekend was about her and her alone. A smile spread across his lips as he watched that little mouth pucker and suckle as she dreamed of nursing. He wondered if she sensed on some level that her life had changed, if she understood that strangers cared for her now. Though the baby had certainly taken to Shana, no question, he couldn't help thinking that the little one knew something wasn't as it should be.

But so far it hadn't affected her sleeping or eating habits. Keith was thankful for that. More than anything else he wanted this baby safe and happy. He'd helped numerous patients, young and old, over the years, but this time was different. It was almost personal. Hit far too close to home.

Something Jaron had said to him suddenly surfaced. "How long have you and Annabelle been friends?" Keith ventured, feeling like a traitor to the standoffish doctor even as he spoke. He was loyal to the hospital and its outstanding staff. That he would give even a whiff of credence to Jaron's suggestion that Annabelle was hiding something was out of line and he knew it. But the baby...

"I don't know, a few months. Not long. We're really not all that close." Shana looked at Keith, a question in her eyes. "She's very protective of her privacy. Why do you ask?"

He thought about stopping the discussion right there, but Shana was in this, too. He wasn't going to hold out on her where the baby was concerned.

"Jaron seems to think Annabelle is hiding something regarding Chris's mother."

Clearly indignant, Shana huffed, "You're kidding, right?"

"Afraid not." Maintaining eye contact was too distracting, so he focused his gaze on the water and the red-and-white fishing floats there. "Apparently the mother said something to Annabelle before she died, and Jaron believes Annabelle is withholding that information."

"That's ridiculous," Shana argued. "She wouldn't do that. We may not have known each other all that long, but I know she's not that kind of person." Her gaze fell on the sleeping infant in the car seat. "She wouldn't do that to the baby." Shana looked at Keith then, waiting for him to meet her eyes. "If she knew anything at all that would help this baby, she would say so."

Shana's conviction intrigued him. Made him like what he saw all the more. But she was running away from something—he could feel it. At the same time, she was after something. He could feel that, too. Keith turned toward the water once more. He didn't care for hidden agendas.

"I can't believe you'd think that of her," Shana said hotly when he remained silent. Despite the anger she'd felt at the question, she remembered to keep her voice low so as not to disturb the baby. How could he believe such a thing about Annabelle? It just couldn't be true. She cared too much about her work and was more dedicated than any doctor Shana had ever known.

"I didn't say I thought she was hiding something," Keith said flatly, not even sparing her a glance. "I said that Jaron believes it."

"Well, he's wrong." She shifted, the whole idea making her restless. "He's wrong," she repeated.

"What made you decide against nursing?"

The question, so far off the subject, startled her from her irritated musings. "What?"

"Nursing. According to your personnel file, you started out in nursing, but then changed your focus to early childhood education."

What had he been doing, looking at her personnel file? "Why—"

Before she could demand an answer, he gave her one. "When Round the Clock was started, it was my job to review all the personnel files along with Human Resources to make sure everyone employed there was up to hospital standards. After all, the center was going to be providing care for the children of staff members as well as some patients. I don't take chances where patient care—any of it—is concerned."

Okay, she supposed that was an appropriate enough explanation. Her irritation faded a bit. Now that she thought about it, he had mentioned her nursing when they first agreed to this weekend, but she'd been too rattled to think anything of it. "I realized pretty quickly that nursing wasn't for me," she said simply. As much as she loved helping people, emotionally she just couldn't handle the job. She couldn't keep herself in professional mode. She'd been forced to admit that her emotions ruled her, and that wasn't a good nursing qualification. "I couldn't keep my emotions out of the equation," she clarified when that relentless gaze wouldn't let her go. Dealing with her mother's extended illness had driven that point home in a big way. "Taking care of children is much more my forte." She smiled down at the baby sleeping between them. "I love children."

"Then why haven't you married and had some of your own?"

Her head came up and her gaze locked with his. Oddly, he seemed just as startled by the question as she was.

She shrugged indifferently, using the moment to school her emotions. "I don't know. I guess I haven't met the right guy." She looked away then, unable to bear that intense gaze boring into her a second longer.

"That's a cliché," he mumbled. "You can't come up with a better excuse than that?"

Now she was ticked off. How was it he knew just the right thing to say to make her madder than all get-out? "Do I need an excuse? Are you one of those guys who think all women should be married and with child by twenty-five? Surely you're a more progressive thinker than that." She made a sound of disbelief. "Besides, it's not like you have any room to talk. Why aren't *you* married?"

Keith knew he'd touched on something with the question. He narrowed his gaze at her. "I get it," he said knowingly, clearly sending her temper flaring again. He could read every emotion on that animated face, in those expressive brown eyes, no matter how she tried to hide them. "It's that trust thing." She'd said she didn't trust him. He was nearly certain someone in her past had betrayed her somehow, hurt her badly. He clenched his jaw instinctively at the thought. What man would hurt a woman like this?

He blinked, startled by that last thought.

"Who says I have trust issues?" she snapped, then glanced at the baby and lowered her voice. "I don't have *any* issues."

Time out, he railed at himself silently. This was supposed to be a relaxing outing. He shouldn't be drilling her about her past again.

"Sorry I asked," he admitted, however grudgingly. It annoyed him that the need to know more about her very nearly outweighed his reasonable side. "Let's talk about something else." *Like sex,* the devil in him added.

"No."

He jerked his head in her direction. "What?"

"Let's talk about trust issues," she retorted. "You lost your mother when you were a child, and were dragged from home to home for months afterward. That's why you won't commit to one woman, Mr.

Hewitt,'' she concluded smugly. ''You're the one with trust issues.''

Fury bolted through him. ''Maybe I just like playing the field,'' he said with clenched teeth. ''Or maybe I simply haven't found the right woman yet.'' He tossed the excuse she had used back at her.

She smiled facetiously. ''It's not for any lack of trying, I understand.''

There she went again with his social life. ''I don't understand this fascination you have with my sex life.'' He kept his voice hushed, but his tone was accusatory and to the point. ''Perhaps you feel left out.''

Her mouth dropped open and she glared at him with utter disdain for two beats before retorting, ''Don't flatter yourself.''

He started to say more, but just then her pole jerked. She gave a little shriek and clutched at it. Her float had disappeared from sight.

''You've got one,'' he muttered as he set his own pole aside to assist her. ''Let me help you.''

By the time they dragged the fish in, they were standing side by side a few feet away from little Chris, who'd slept through the whole event.

''Oh, my God,'' Shana exclaimed. ''My first fish.'' She looked at the flailing catch and beamed a smile.

''You'll enjoy it all the more because you caught it yourself.''

Her smile drooped into a ground-dragging frown. ''You expect me to eat it?''

He laughed. ''Well, yeah. You ate the ones I caught yesterday.''

Her face puckered up like a petulant child's. "But that was different. I hadn't seen those while they still had scales and—and a head." She looked sympathetically toward the wriggling animal. "I can't eat this fish. He's...he's real. Alive." She shoved the pole at Keith. "Put it back."

"You can't—"

"Put it back!" she repeated, forcefully emphasizing each word.

And that was the way it went. Later that morning, when they returned to the cabin, they carried only the baby, the carrier and the fishing poles. By unspoken mutual consent, mainly for the sake of little Chris, they'd returned to neutral territory as far as their personal disagreements went.

The message alert was blinking furiously on the answering machine when they entered the cabin. While Shana fed and changed the baby, Keith pressed the button and listened to the message. It was Seth Nannery giving Keith a heads-up that Detective Jaron Dorsey and Dr. Annabelle Peters were on their way out to the cabin to check on the baby and to take photographs of her for identification purposes.

That told Keith something he'd just as soon not have heard: the baby's identity was still a mystery....

KEITH AND SHANA, holding Chris, stepped out onto the front deck as Annabelle's odd little yellow car braked to a stop in the drive next to Keith's SUV.

Harold, Annabelle's sixteen-year-old golden retriever, shot out of the car and bounded off into the woods as if he'd suddenly gained a new lease on life.

"You guys only need coonskin caps, rocking chairs and a banjo to make a perfect picture," Annabelle announced with an uncharacteristic smile.

Shana grinned and hurried down the steps to meet her friend. Keith was right behind her.

"I left the coonskin inside," he said jovially. "On the rocking chair. And if I produce the banjo, this good woman here would likely head for the hills so fast we wouldn't see her again anytime soon."

This good woman. He couldn't be talking about her, Shana thought, but he was. She had never heard him speak like that before, at least not where she was concerned. She was surprised, to say the least, at his sudden playfulness. Was it just a show to cover the tension? Did he worry that Annabelle or Detective Dorsey wouldn't approve of their caring for Chris if they were hostile toward each other? They'd pretty much ignored conversation and one another since returning from the creek. What was going on inside that head of his now?

Only God knew. Shana didn't have the first clue.

Annabelle looked as if she were trying to grasp the whole picture herself. Her gaze shifted from Shana to Keith and back. *Oh, Lord,* Shana thought abruptly. *Please don't let her see the other thing brewing between us.* Shana definitely didn't want to become known as Keith Hewitt's latest conquest.

Keith moved toward the detective, his shoulder inadvertently brushing hers. Shana's breath caught before she could stop it. Heat infused her cheeks and she realized there was no way Annabelle could have missed the little hitch in her breathing.

"Did Seth tell you why we've come?" Jaron Dorsey asked.

Shana knew why they were here. To help little Chris. She smiled down at the tiny angel.

"He said that Annabelle would be coming in the capacity of helpful hospital employee and photographer for Chris." Keith turned to Jaron and grinned. "I suppose you're here to make sure it's all done legally."

"Chris?" Annabelle echoed.

"She arrived on Columbus Day weekend," Keith quickly explained, before Shana had a chance to speak up. "In the absence of any other name, Shana dubbed her Chris." He shrugged. "Seems sort of appropriate."

Annabelle moved closer to Shana and peered down at the baby in her arms.

"Chris," she said. "It's perfect." The doctor caressed the baby's face. "Is she feeding well?"

"Both ends are operating very satisfactorily," Shana said pointedly. "I think we're going to run out of diapers before this weekend is over." She traced one soft little cheek with the tip of her finger. "The way this one goes through 'em makes me almost feel guilty for not using cloth diapers." She shot her host a look that said someone was going to have to make a trip into town. "But it's just as well that we don't have the cloth ones, since Keith here doesn't have a washing machine.''

"We have dish towels," Keith said dryly. "We could always use those. Besides, this is the West, my dear. Wild West women made do without washing machines.''

Boy, he was really getting into this little charade. *Dear.* What was that about? "Okay, Billy the Kid," she retorted. "After we've used a few of those dish towels, you take your coonskin cap and a bagful of those makeshift diapers down to the creek for washing.''

"You must be kidding," he countered. "The EPA would be on us like flies on—"

"I get the picture," Shana said quickly. "How about you trot off to town and buy another box of the disposable kind.''

"Your wish is my command," he said with a slight bow. "Just say when.''

Shana shook herself. This was truly…strange. She turned her attention to their visitors, who looked almost as startled as she felt. "Do you two have time for coffee? We have leftover muffins that Keith made for breakfast this morning.''

"Keith—muffins?" Annabelle stammered.

"There's no need to look so stunned," Keith argued, sounding injured. He turned to Jaron. "We modern-day males can do almost anything, don't you agree?''

Jaron only grinned at Keith and then turned to Annabelle. "What about it, Dr. Peters? Do we have time for a muffin by Chef Hewitt?''

Annabelle was shaking her head before he finished the question. Shana was disappointed at her response. She'd hoped they would stay awhile. She definitely needed the cushion of other human beings. Things were changing far too rapidly around here.

"We'll just take the pictures and be on our way," Annabelle insisted, her tone suddenly cool. "I have things I need to do this afternoon, and I'm sure all of you do, as well."

"So be it," Jaron said, but Shana didn't miss the disappointment in his voice. She wasn't the only one who wanted to hold on to the moment. She wondered, though, what Jaron's motivation was.

Shana unwrapped the bunny blanket from around Chris and offered her to Jaron.

"Okay, sweetheart," he said softly, "let's get you documented for posterity and let these very busy people get on with their very busy lives. Then maybe you can go back to the important things in the world—like sleeping."

Again Shana heard a note of indefinable emotion in his voice. Sadness maybe, or defeat. She wondered about that. She looked from Jaron to Annabelle. Was there something going on here? Or maybe it was simply her own guilt over this crazy infatuation with Keith that had her imposing the same on their colleagues. Misery loved company.

Whatever it was, there was an underlying tension about the scene that needed to be broken. And Shana knew just how to do that.

WITH SOME PRODDING, the picture shoot went beautifully, almost magically. Even Harold enjoyed the frolic. Actually, Shana amended, he seemed to enjoy it most of all.

Annabelle handled the camera as if she were a trained professional. Shana wondered if this was her hobby. Though they'd been friends for a while, this was the first time she'd seen her with a camera. But now that Shana thought about it, she recalled all those photographs in Annabelle's apartment. She'd just never put two and two together, and any personal information had to be pulled out of Annabelle as if she were guarding some national secret. Shana wished the doctor would open up a bit more to her.

What made the day was the quiet serenity of the creek. Shana insisted they do the picture-taking there. The soft grass along the bank was still green, and she had thoroughly enjoyed their time at the creek that morning, worms aside.

For the shoot, Shana held the baby first, while Annabelle snapped away. Then Keith took a turn. He seemed far more ready to jump into the act than Shana would have expected. It was so peculiar. His behavior almost seemed surreal…as if he were overacting.

"Look!" He held the baby up for all to see. "She smiled!"

They'd all tried different methods to bring about a smile. Jaron was particularly good at making sounds and faces that would appeal to children. He had the most experience, Shana reasoned, having two children of his own. But little Chris had staunchly ignored all their attempts. Until now...

"It's likely gas," Annabelle proclaimed.

Good-naturedly, Shana, Keith and Jaron simultaneously argued otherwise, then they all looked at each other and laughed.

"Gas!" Shana stifled her chuckles. "I don't think so!" Stepping closer to the baby in Keith's arms, she cooed soft sounds and the smile widened. "Look at that beautiful smile! Isn't it the most precious thing you've ever seen?"

Keith was looking at her strangely now. Shana blinked and backed up a step. Maybe she'd gotten too close. Or maybe he was uncomfortable holding the baby with everyone making such a fuss. But a few minutes ago he'd been right in the thick of it himself.

"You should hold her." Shana turned to Jaron, forcing her attention away from Keith. "It'll be perfect," she said to Annabelle. "Seth will get his sympathetic headlines with that one. Injured Officer Holds Orphaned Baby." She suddenly remembered his bandages from the other night, when he'd picked up his kids at Round the Clock. "Jaron, where are your big bulky bandages?"

"I don't need bandages," he said sternly. "I agreed to keep this layer of gauze on, though, because it allows me to still use my hands."

Men, she mused. Always had to play the part of a tough guy. Annabelle's expression seemed to second Shana's thought.

Then Shana smiled with inspiration. "Wait—I've

got it! Heroic Injured Cop Holds Orphaned Baby. What a guy!''

Keith offered the baby to Jaron, who looked uncertain but finally took the squirming infant.

''Annabelle, get this,'' Shana urged. ''Hero and baby. It's perfect.''

Annabelle smiled, too, but the expression didn't reach her eyes. Even more disturbing, Shana thought she saw the woman's fingers tremble as she took aim with the camera. Annabelle was starting to behave as strangely as Keith.

Silence ensued for five long beats, with no telltale click of the shutter.

''I…'' Annabelle lowered the camera without taking the picture. ''Surely we have enough shots now.''

''I'll take this one.'' Keith stepped forward and tugged the camera from Annabelle's hand. ''Just one more,'' he cajoled. ''Doctor and cop—the team who saved the baby and who desperately tried to save the mother.'' Although his expression had turned jovial again, his words were solemn.

''Go ahead,'' he urged when Annabelle didn't move. ''Stand next to Jaron and the baby. Seth will love it. Maybe you can hold Chris,'' he added.

Annabelle accepted the baby into her arms with more than a little reluctance. ''He's right,'' Shana said, supporting Keith's suggestion and hoping to set Annabelle at ease. ''It'll be perfect.''

But Annabelle didn't look convinced. Still, she surrendered to the majority vote, looking stiff and uncomfortable. ''It's not an automatic camera,'' she suddenly said to Keith. There was something helpless in her tone, as if she'd have given anything to be behind the camera instead of in front of it.

Shana analyzed that thought for a second. Did her friend prefer to watch life rather than participate? Shana had been guilty of the same thing herself. She definitely couldn't pass judgment on anyone else. Her attention settled on Jaron and then Keith. Considering what Keith had told her about himself, as well as Jaron, she imagined that all four of them were guilty of avoiding life to some degree.

What a shame…

The moment went downhill from there.

No matter how Shana tried to lighten the mood, things just kept growing tenser between Annabelle and Jaron. Maybe it was as Keith had suggested. Maybe Jaron did believe Annabelle was hiding something.

Then again, maybe they were suffering from the same ailment that was plaguing Shana—desperate attraction for the wrong person.

Keith Hewitt was the last man on the planet she should be lusting after.

She shook her head as she watched Annabelle and Jaron drive away, with Harold staring wistfully out the back.

Life could be really confusing sometimes. She cuddled the baby close to her heart. At times it could be downright heartbreaking.

If only we could know what lies in store for us, she mused silently. But only God knew.

She peered down at the sweet infant in her arms and prayed that God was looking out for her. Baby Chris needed his help most of all.

Turning, Shana started up the steps to the cabin and found Keith leaning in the doorway, watching her. His hair was mussed from the breeze, and those amber eyes were studying her, making her restless and too hot inside her own skin. Broad shoulders tested the seams of his blue chambray shirt. Those wide shoulders tapered to a lean waist, narrow hips and long, jean-clad legs. She had to look away.

Quickly, silently, she amended her prayer with a plea for herself. It was going to take an act of God to keep her out of the trouble her heart was racing to get her into.

CHAPTER NINE

KEITH AWOKE WITH A START.

He lay in the darkness for several seconds, trying to determine what had awakened him.

The baby, crying...

Remembering that first night when Shana had been ill, he bolted from the bed and headed to her room, hopping on one foot and then the other as he tugged on his jeans.

To his relief, Shana appeared to be fine.

While making comforting shushing sounds, she paced the length of the room with the baby cradled in her arms.

The second observation Keith made concerned the way Shana was dressed. The nightgown wasn't the generic nightshirt she'd been wearing the first time he was awakened by a howling infant. No, this was definitely different. This garment looked silky and barely hit her midthigh. He swallowed with difficulty. It was jade in color and flattered her slender figure. And, oh yes, she had terrific legs. Amazing legs.

Not until she turned around and halted in her tracks did he realize that he'd been staring openmouthed—mostly at those long, shapely legs. He tried to meet her eyes, but his gaze was waylaid where the distracting fabric molded to her heavy breasts, leaving just the right amount of cleavage visible to tantalize him.

"She just won't go to sleep," Shana said helplessly. "I've done everything I know to do and nothing works."

Keith jerked himself from the haze of lust and zeroed in on those big brown eyes. "Do we need to call Annabelle?" His heart kicked into a higher gear. What if the baby was sick? They had stayed outside a lot today, with the fishing and then the visit with Jaron and Annabelle. What if the outdoor air had been too much for a newborn? He sure as heck didn't know about things like that. But wouldn't Annabelle have said something? A wave of hysteria raced through him. What if they'd done something wrong?

Shana stared at the fretful baby for a time, then sighed. "I don't really think we need a doctor. Chrissy doesn't have a fever and she took her bottle like she was starved." Shana shook her head and resumed pacing. "I don't think she's ill. It's something else. She's just fighting sleep. Babies do that sometimes, but I can't help worrying."

He scrubbed at his brow. "What can I do?"

She shrugged. "I don't know. I…"

She looked ready to drop. She needed to sit down, that much was apparent. He'd been so busy admiring her in that sensual slip of pure torment that he'd failed to notice her obvious fatigue. The dark smudges beneath her eyes, the exhaustion evident in the slight slump of her shoulders…

"I'll take over for a while." He met her in the middle of the room and took the baby before she could argue.

Little Chris wriggled, and those tiny lips puckered as if she might let out a wail of protest. But Keith lifted her to his shoulder and softly patted her backside before she could.

"Shh," he whispered as he started the pacing ritual himself, while rhythmically patting her diaper-clad bottom. She rubbed her little face against his bare shoulder, and Keith couldn't help but smile. She felt so good against him like this. So warm and precious...so fragile. It amazed him all over again just how wonderful it was to hold a baby. He'd never expected to feel this way.

The baby settled quickly, those tiny lips moving against his skin as if searching, even in her sleep, for something to nurse. His chest constricted and he could scarcely draw a breath. What power this little girl had over him.

Shana had dropped into a chair by the bed, her expression nothing short of stunned. That should have made him angry—the idea that she would think him lacking the necessary compassion to help with the baby—but it didn't. He just didn't have the energy to work up the emotion. Or was it something else that kept him from feeling angry?

Keith didn't allow his gaze to linger on Shana however. That would only get him into trouble. The idea of just how much control these two females had over him scared the hell out of him. He resisted the urge to shake his head when he considered what an imbecile he'd acted like today while Jaron and Annabelle visited. Everything he'd said and done had come out the wrong way. He'd been going for nonchalant, not wanting the others to pick up on the tension simmering between him and Shana. But what had he done? He'd acted like a complete fool.

Judging by the looks of confusion on all three faces, they'd gotten a pretty damn good picture of how sadly out of control he was.

And that kiss. His senses instantly replayed every second of that mind-blowing event.

He forced himself to take long, slow, deep breaths to offset the desire heating up inside him. Even with the baby in his arms, he couldn't keep his mind off Shana.

What was he supposed to do when this was over? How would he ever work in the same hospital with this woman and not do anything totally stupid?

"Don't you think she knows?"

The question brought him up short and he turned to the woman who'd spoken.

"Knows what?" The baby, he reminded himself. She was talking about the baby. For just one second there he feared she'd read his mind.

"That her parents are gone forever." Shana pushed up from the chair, simultaneously running a hand through those sexy, bed-mussed auburn locks. "That something is very wrong."

She paused near him, which sent his senses to an even higher state of alert. "I don't know," he managed to say, though he couldn't hide the distracted quality in his tone. "Possibly. I'm sure she realizes she's with strangers…though she's adapted well." A frown inched across his brow. "Quite well."

Shana sighed tiredly, drawing his attention once more to those luscious breasts. "Do you think Annabelle and Jaron's visit upset her? Could she have associated their voices with that day?"

Keith blinked, focusing fully on the question. He hadn't thought of that. It was possible, he supposed. Jaron's voice was the first the baby had heard after the tragedy…and then Annabelle's.

"Maybe," he allowed. "She would probably remember their voices."

"But would she know that those voices were somehow connected to all these sudden changes?" Shana massaged her temple with the fingers of her right hand. "Could she sense that and be troubled by it?"

The whole idea had Shana extremely upset. Keith patted the baby's softly padded bottom once more, noting that she continued to sleep soundly. Thank God.

But Shana was far from settled. He reached out to her then. Couldn't help himself. "I can't answer that," he said gently. His fingers wrapped around the velvety smooth softness of her forearm, and a shard of need sliced straight through him. "It's possible, I guess. Then again, we could be presuming too much. Who knows for certain how much a baby understands or remembers during infancy?"

She nodded resignedly. "I know. It's just that I

can't help thinking that the visit upset her—made her restless.''

But Chrissy certainly didn't appear restless now. Shana couldn't believe that the baby had actually gone to sleep nestled against that massive chest. Shana shivered inwardly. She wouldn't mind being nestled there herself. But sleeping definitely wouldn't be on her mind.

The whole picture shook her. Her internal temperature had risen steadily from the moment he'd entered the room wearing nothing but those jeans. That chest…it was simply awesome. Every muscle was masterfully delineated. The good Lord had sure done a fine job doling out remarkable assets to Keith Hewitt. The dark hair scattered across that appealing territory made her want to smooth her palms over the masculine ridges and planes.

The whole tousled, sleepy look was almost more than she could take. He had just climbed out of bed and he looked amazing.

That was only supposed to happen in the movies.

And with that baby in his arms…well, he looked…right.

Too right.

Shana had an almost overwhelming urge to run. This man was more dangerous than she'd first thought. He'd already charmed his way into her heart somehow.

''You think I could put her to bed now?'' he asked quietly, those amber eyes watching Shana closely.

The absolute last thing she needed was for him to realize the depth of the effect he had on her.

''We can try.'' She hurried toward the drawer on the bed that served as a cradle, and readied it for the baby, her movements jerky. The sooner they got Chris settled, the sooner he would go back to his room and leave her to her personal torture of forbidden fantasies.

Even before the baby had started fretting, Shana had lain in bed, unable to sleep as she thought of how much she wanted to know Keith on the most intimate of levels. She closed her eyes now and read herself the riot act. How could she be so stupid?

He would only break her heart.

No matter what she thought she saw or felt, he was not as vulnerable as she was. He would take whatever he could and walk away without permanent damage. She, on the other hand, would never get over losing him. She knew it with as much certainty as she knew her own shoe size.

When the baby was tucked in and it became apparent she would sleep, Shana led the way into the hall so their talking wouldn't interfere with that blessed slumber.

''Thanks for coming to my rescue again,'' she said in all sincerity. This was the second time he'd jumped in and taken charge, ultimately saving the day. She had, apparently, been wrong about him…at least about some parts.

''Why wouldn't I?'' The question came out a little defensively.

"I don't mean it like that," she hastened to explain. He'd definitely misunderstood her. "I just meant that—"

"I'm not the fatherly type?"

That question was a *lot* defensive.

She shook her head. "Keith, I only meant—"

He held up both hands. "I know what you meant." He exhaled a heavy breath. "I guess I'm just a little on edge."

That was a relief. She didn't want to argue with him, though it might help keep some distance. "I guess I just got all upset thinking that maybe our company today made the baby relive the horror of…" She lifted a shoulder in a semblance of a shrug. "Well, you know."

He reached out to her again, and fire shot straight through her body. How she managed to keep the reaction an inward one, she would never know.

"The baby's going to be fine. We're going to see to it. We can't change what's happened, but we can see that she gets off to a fresh start."

Shana nodded. "I know." And the baby was lucky to have them. Shana knew that, too. This was a personal sacrifice for both of them. Her gaze connected fully with his. Especially for him.

"It was truly awful, wasn't it?"

She didn't have to clarify. Somehow he instinctively knew that she was no longer talking about Chris, but was inquiring about him and his past.

For a long moment he looked so deeply into her eyes that she was certain he didn't intend to answer.

In that time she watched the emotions dance across his face. The denial, the anger, the defeat.

"It was…yes, it was truly awful."

He fell silent for a long moment, his fingers still curled loosely around her wrist. Shana could only watch the transformation taking place right in front of her. He was opening up, making himself vulnerable. And he was touching her, connecting with her in a way that went well beyond the mere physical. A part of her rejoiced, but another part, a saner part, tensed, knowing that she was skating on thin ice here.

"The fear is something I can't explain." His gaze grew distant, and she knew that he was no longer seeing *her,* but something from his past. "All that you depend on is suddenly torn away from you. There's no one you can rely on…no one you know to trust. It's the single worst feeling…."

The silence that followed was not uncomfortable, and it felt necessary somehow. "I won't let that happen to her," he said at last, his focus returning, his eyes glittering with golden fire. "It's going to be different for her."

And just like that, Shana's battle was lost. She put her arms around him and pressed her cheek to that warm, smooth chest just as little Chris had. Shana had to comfort him somehow, had to hold him. For one long, breathless moment she feared he would push her away, but eventually his arms came around her and she felt complete at last.

"I'm sorry," she murmured, her lips reveling in

the feel of his bare skin beneath them. "I'm so sorry that happened to you."

Those firm lips of his pressed against her hair, and her arms tightened instinctively around him. The feel of his heart beating somehow soothed her, made her want to stay right here in his arms forever.

His hands started to move over her back, caressing, exploring, making her breath catch. God, it felt so right to be with him like this. His exploration urged her on, and she smoothed her palms over his strong back, the feel of hard muscle making her feminine core burn with need. She shouldn't allow this, but she wanted it...wanted it now. Unable to hold back, she turned her face into his chest and kissed the hot flesh there. He groaned savagely and his hands became more desperate, moving over her more frantically.

But it was the feel of his sex hardening that undid her completely. He wanted her just as much as she wanted him. Those searching hands molded to her bottom, pressed her more intimately to him, and her ability to breathe ceased entirely.

His mouth sought hers and captured it, and that skilled tongue delved inside with such tenderness and need that she felt certain her heart could not take the sweetness of it. He lifted her fully against him and carried her to the bed where he'd been sleeping.

She told herself to resist, but somehow the message just wouldn't go through. She wanted this...wanted it as desperately as he seemed to.

He lowered her to the bed, never allowing his body to lose contact with hers. The smoothness of his skin, the rougher texture of his jeans, the incredible heat he emanated—there were so many sensations…. The feel of his hair between her fingers as she urged on his kiss, the hot taste of his mouth. She wanted more. To feel all of him…taste all of him.

The fresh scent of soap and something uniquely his filled her as she inhaled deeply between kisses. Need exploded anew inside her, making her tremble.

Keith couldn't think…he could only feel. Shana was on fire—her soft skin so hot it very nearly burned his fingertips. He nudged one knee between those long legs and prepared to nestle himself right where he wanted to be. Her wicked tongue dueled with his, giving him back as good as he gave. He'd known it would be this way. She was every bit as animated in bed as she was—

He stopped, his pulse pounding so loudly in his ears he could scarcely think. His entire body bordered on the edge of orgasm. He drew back and his gaze collided with hers. Reality crashed in on him like a roof giving way under the weight of heavy snow.

He had her in his bed and was on the verge of making love to her, just as he'd dreamed of for days or maybe even weeks now. No matter how he attempted to deny it, he'd been subconsciously fantasizing about her ever since he'd met her.

She blinked, those wide eyes suddenly clouded with confusion and uncertainty.

She was as eager as he was, but this couldn't happen. She wanted…something. Something he felt sure he couldn't give her. And he wanted nothing more than *this*—no strings. The one thing he knew about Shana with utter certainty was that she was not a no-strings kind of woman. She would want the whole nine yards. The wedding, white picket fence, children. Images of her holding Chris flashed through his mind, underscoring what he had already figured out about her.

Shana Devlin wanted more than he could give. That's why he'd subconsciously done all within his power to keep distance between them. That's why they had clashed at every turn from the moment she'd arrived in Seattle.

Rather than risk giving in, he'd kept her at bay the only way he knew how.

Until now...

"We can't do this," he muttered. Ignoring the raging protest of his entire body, he pushed himself up from the bed and moved a few feet away, leaving her lying there, dazed and thoroughly confused. And so damn beautiful he could hardly bear to look at her.

She scrambled up from the twisted sheets. Righting the tiny straps of her slinky gown, she glanced around the room, clearly grappling for what to say in response to his turnabout. God, he was a complete heel.

She would hate him for this.

But it was the best thing for both of them.

Shaking her head, she stared up at him. "We have to talk about this." She flung her arms outward in exasperation. "This is...this has got to stop." She smoothed her hands down her silky gown as if she feared it revealed too much. "I didn't intend for things to go this far.'' She blinked but kept her gaze fixed firmly on his. ''I only meant to comfort you. I…''

That she would deny what he knew she'd felt, what he was certain she'd wanted, sent his emotions plunging toward anger. ''I'm not blind, Shana,'' he growled. ''I know what you wanted. You wanted the same thing I did.''

Lifting that delicate chin in defiance, she glared at him. ''Okay, so what if I'm attracted to you? Isn't every female on the planet? You're good-looking, sexy. Why wouldn't I be attracted to you? But that doesn't mean I wanted—'' she glanced at the bed ''—this.''

All she had to do was look, and she would see just how much he wanted the same thing. ''It felt like you did,'' he charged.

She shoved the hair back from her face. ''I just got caught up in the moment. That's all.''

He rolled his eyes. ''Fine. Then let's call it a night and forget about the whole thing.''

''Fine.'' She glared at him one last time before stomping out of the room.

He puffed out a breath and tamped down the urge to go after her and make her admit the truth. She'd wanted him. End of story.

But what would that accomplish?

Nothing.

The baby was asleep and that's all that mattered.

He climbed back into his bed and clicked off the

bedside lamp. Let her believe what she would. He knew what he'd felt.

Closing his eyes, he concentrated on forcing his body to relax—something that might just take all night.

SHANA COULD NOT BELIEVE the audacity of the man!

She slipped into bed, careful not to disturb the sleeping infant.

How could he lie on the other side of this wall— she glared up at the offending partition—and pretend she'd meant to let things get so carried away? Yes, she definitely had wanted him. But she hadn't set out to end up in bed with him. She closed her eyes and allowed the sensations to wash over her once more. The feel of his hands on her body. The taste of his skin. The hard male contours against her softer feminine peaks and valleys. The way he controlled the kiss, making her breathless…

She'd forgotten all about the scared little boy she'd wanted to comfort, and had focused body and soul on the hard, hungry man in her arms.

She shivered in spite of her intention to put him out of her mind. The task was simply impossible.

ON THE OTHER SIDE of the thin wall, Keith tossed and turned. He couldn't stop thinking about the way Shana had felt beneath him. His entire being longed to touch her again…to taste her again. But his brain told him that would be a mistake. Yet somehow that didn't seem to matter to the rest of him. No other woman had ever felt so right in his arms.

Sure, he'd had mind-boggling sex before. But there was something different about Shana. The heat and intensity was there, but there was a vulnerability, an innocence that blew him totally away.

But she wasn't innocent.

She wanted something. Something he couldn't give.

SHANA ROLLED ONTO her side, tugging the cover up under her chin. Yes, it was true. She knew exactly what she wanted. She wanted a husband and a home. Children, the whole ball of wax. She wanted the fairy tale.

And what was wrong with that?

MARRIAGE, KIDS. There was nothing wrong with that…for the right guy. Keith flopped onto his side and stared at the clock on the bedside table. But he didn't want permanence. He didn't want to fall in love and risk the emotions required for that kind of commitment. How could he bring another life into this world, knowing all the hazards? He couldn't; it was that simple.

From personal experience as well as professional, he knew what could go wrong, and he could not bring himself to knowingly put anyone, much less himself, in that precarious position.

Sex would have to be enough.

SHANA SIGHED. True love was what she wanted; she didn't just want sex. Anyone could have sex for its own sake—what amounted to nothing more than an exercise in self-indulgence.

How dare he accuse her of only wanting sex. Of having so little respect for herself—not to mention him—that she would go that far! She wasn't that kind of girl.

She would not let another minute pass without making him understand how wrong he was on that score.

She eased up and out of the bed. She would just set the record straight right now.

KEITH HEAVED A DISGUSTED breath. She'd started this whole damn thing, anyway, by putting her arms around him. Then she'd blamed him for almost taking what she offered. He sat up and swung his legs over the edge of the bed. That was just like Shana Devlin, teasing and tempting.

The next time she pushed him that close to the edge he was going to finish it.

He might as well warn her now.

Another episode like tonight's would not be tolerated. He stormed out of his room, intent on calling her out for that *talk* she'd insisted they have.

Keith drew up short, almost bumping into Shana in the hall. "What're you doing up?" he demanded, flustered that she'd startled him. How the hell could this woman keep him so unsteady on his feet?

"What're *you* doing up?" she retorted, hands on

hips, forcing that sensuous fabric to mold more closely to her pelvis.

God, he wanted her.

He shook off that thought. "Just so you know," he said hotly, "the next time you start this thing between us, I'm going to finish it once and for all."

Those brown eyes narrowed accusingly. "I didn't start anything. You did."

He considered arguing the point, but it would be useless. "Think what you will," he snapped. "But know this. I'd be more than happy to have sex with you if that's what you want. Just don't expect more."

She looked at him as if he'd slapped her. "Excuse me?"

He pointed a finger at her to emphasize his words. "I know what you want, Shana Devlin, and you won't find it here. If you're hunting for a husband, you've come to the wrong place. Now…" he settled a look on her that left no question as to what he meant "…if you're searching for great sex, well then, that's another story."

THE WORDS SLAMMED into Shana, instantly producing white-hot fury. She opened her mouth to lash out at him, but then another thought surfaced, made her think before she spoke. She had his number, all right. She should have realized it before. The knowledge made her smile, but did nothing to lessen the tempest roaring through her.

"Admit it, Hewitt," she challenged. "You're afraid of me."

He laughed, but the sound was strained.

She'd hit the mark. So that was his problem.

"You're afraid of commitment, and a girl like me makes you wish you weren't." She folded her arms over her chest and reveled in her triumph. Oh, yes, she had his number now.

"I'm not afraid of anything," he said fiercely, his glower almost making her take a step back. "I'm certainly not afraid of a woman who's so obviously *obsessed* with commitment, and brings it up with every breath."

A tremor of vulnerability went through her, but this had gone too far to stop now. "Fine, I'll admit my weakness if you'll admit yours." She squared her shoulders and stared directly into those accusing eyes. "Yes, I want a husband and family. I want it all. Why not?"

Her confession surprised him, gave him pause. It was easy to see that he wasn't sure what to say to that. Indecision was written all over his face.

"But you don't go looking for it like you really want it," he countered finally. Something new was in his eyes now, a kind of anxiety she hadn't seen before. "All you do is talk about it."

"I just have to be sure, that's all." She trembled from the weight of her own emotions. She hated that the anger had drained away, leaving her susceptible to these softer, weaker feelings. "When I make a commitment, I want it to be real…and to last."

His eyes flashed, hot and intense. "Tell me, Shana." When she would have turned away, he grabbed her by the arms and made her look at him. "Who let you down? There had to be someone who hurt you." He pulled her nearer, putting those tempting lips directly in line with hers. "I'm not the only one shying away from commitment. Talk is cheap."

She could feel his warm breath on her lips as he spoke again, more softly now, but no less urgently. "Tell me," he urged, "who let you down so badly?"

She wanted to push him away—she really did. But she couldn't find the strength. She didn't want to answer, but she couldn't help herself. "Everyone I ever counted on," she murmured, the admission bringing the sting of tears to her eyes. "Are you satisfied now?"

He shook his head, the movement barely discernible. And then he kissed her. Kissed her so long and so deeply that her knees buckled. But he caught her and pulled her against himself as if he could protect her from the pain twisting through her, right along with the desire.

"I don't know what you do to me," he whispered against her lips, his breath ragged from the kiss, "but you make me want things I've never wanted before."

She touched his mouth with her fingertips, traced the lips that could kiss her as no one else had. "This is crazy," she protested weakly. "We don't even like each other."

That hooded gaze focused on her lips while she spoke, as if he intended to kiss her again. "That's the part I don't get...." He cupped her face in one hand, caressed her cheek with his thumb. "But I just can't help myself."

The granitelike condition of his body verified his every word.

"We should get some sleep." With monumental effort she backed out of his arms. She couldn't let this get out of control again. "I'm not sure either one of us is thinking straight."

He cleared his throat. "You're right. We shouldn't—" he shook his head and retreated a step "—do anything rash."

She hugged herself, her body reeling from the loss of his arms around her. God, how she wanted this man. But it would be a huge mistake. Sex was the only thing he wanted. And it wouldn't mean to him what it would to her.

"Good night then." She turned and took another step away from him, barely resisting the urge to run.

"Shana."

She stilled, her heart pounding so hard she was certain he must hear it. The sound of her name on his lips shifted something deep inside her, and made her heart skip a beat. When she faced him, looked into those eyes, she saw the same battle she fought taking place in him.

"Good night," he murmured.

For one eternal second she was certain he intended to say more, then he walked away.

Shana watched him disappear into his room. She'd told him everything, admitted her deepest secret. And he'd shown a kind of understanding and tenderness in response.

Could she have been looking for the right man all this time and not have known he was there in front of her? That couldn't possibly be the case. Keith wanted nothing to do with commitment. And they hated each other.

Didn't they?

She released a heavy breath and went back to her room. Now there were two mysteries to solve.

The identity of Baby Chris, and figuring out just what this thing between Keith and her really was.

For the baby's sake, she hoped the first would be solved soon. But the second...well, she wasn't sure that either she or Keith was fully prepared for that mystery to be unraveled.

CHAPTER TEN

MONDAY MORNING FOUND Keith with a whole new outlook. He had decided that cabin fever was the cause of all his problems. His strange behavior had nothing to do with Shana personally, it was simply the forced proximity. They'd been enemies for as long as they'd known each other, and being stuck within the same four walls for the last fifty or sixty hours was playing havoc with his ability to reason.

She was, after all, a woman—a beauty at that. He was a hot-blooded male. Of course the attraction would sizzle. He'd have to be dead not to notice those remarkable curves and that kiss-me mouth. Those big brown eyes and the delicate curve of her cheek...

Arousal was instantaneous.

He cursed himself and reached for the cup of coffee he'd poured and forgotten about the moment she traipsed into his thoughts.

He was wrong, he admitted reluctantly. It wasn't just the proximity—he was definitely losing it. As soon as he returned to the city, he would need to get checked out. At the very least he had to be suffering from some sort of chemical imbalance. Either that or he needed a straitjacket.

He didn't need a wife. What's more, he didn't want a wife.

Just then Shana floated down the stairs. He froze, unable to move a muscle as his eyes took in the way she filled out her jeans, and the way the soft texture of her sweater hugged those tantalizing breasts. His fingers tightened on the mug in his hand until he feared it might crack.

Her gaze met his and she smiled. His heart fluttered madly in his chest. Those rosy lips parted, showing off straight white teeth, and her dark eyes brightened as if she were immensely glad to see him.

And just like that, all reason left him.

"Good morning," she said cheerily. "Thanks for letting me sleep in." She glanced at the baby sleeping soundly in her drawer-turned-cradle on the sofa.

He'd known Shana hadn't gotten enough sleep, so he'd sneaked into her room this morning—the door had been open—and retrieved the baby when he heard her first peep. Shana had slept through it all, proof positive that she'd been exhausted.

It was the right thing to do.

It didn't mean anything.

He set his coffee mug on the counter. "She's had her morning feeding and I actually managed to change her diaper."

Shana leaned down and inspected his work. "I see that."

Okay, so he sucked at getting those tape thingies to stay in place. At least he'd tried, and the baby's bottom was dry.

"There're only a couple left," he commented, hoping to get his mind back on the right track. "There's a general store a few miles toward town. I'll pick up a small box later to get us through until tomorrow." She'd actually mentioned the need for diapers yesterday but he'd forgotten.

She nodded and started toward the kitchen. Keith tensed, then swore at himself for reacting in such a ridiculous manner. Just because he was attracted to her didn't mean anything. He couldn't catch the commitment bug just from being exposed to a woman who suffered from the disease. They were polar opposites. It would never work.

Even if he wanted it to, he added.

And he didn't.

His entire being refuted that pronouncement.

He studiously ignored the mutiny.

"Coffee smells good." She brushed past him and reached for a mug.

His body hardened instantly at the brief contact. He rolled his eyes and resisted the urge to kick himself repeatedly. There had to be a logical explanation for this bizarre behavior. One minute he was certain of what he felt and wanted; the next, he was totally up in the air.

"Hmm, more muffins." She grabbed one and bit into it. "You make the most heavenly muffins, Keith," she said between chews. Her eyes closed and she made a throaty sound of pleasure.

Keith tried to speak but couldn't. He was helpless to do anything but watch that sensuous mouth devour the muffin she held in her fingers. Her every moan of approval jerked at his sanity. When she licked those full lips and smiled up at him, he groaned out loud, couldn't help it.

"You're amazing in a kitchen," she said in a sultry voice that finished yanking the rug right out from under his feet. If she heard his beastly growl, she didn't let on.

Then she poured a cup of coffee and padded on bare feet toward the sofa.

When he had calmed his raging hard-on enough to walk, he took his cooling coffee and joined her, choosing to occupy the chair on the opposite side of the coffee table. This was definitely close enough.

Shana sighed and stared down at the baby. "Tomorrow's the day," she said resignedly.

He knew what she meant. Tomorrow they would return to the hospital, and Baby Chris would have to go into foster care if her next of kin wasn't located by the end of the day. Keith could allow her to stay at the center until then, but no longer. He was already stretching the limits of procedural policy.

"There are some really good foster homes out there," he said, hoping to reassure her. "I'll make certain she goes to the best available." And he would do all he could. He'd already decided that this baby shouldn't suffer any more than she already had.

"But it won't be the same," Shana murmured. She didn't have to look at him for Keith to know that tears had welled in her eyes. He could hear the emotion in her voice.

"Shana," he said softly. She looked at him then, the emotion he'd suspected bright in her eyes. "Chris is an infant. It'll be easy to find a good family for her. It's the older kids who usually have difficulty being fostered."

"Like you did?"

Why did she have to keep bringing that up? He shouldn't have told her. "That's right. Like I did." He stared at his cup, not wanting to see the sympathy that glittered in those wide, expressive orbs. Sympathy for him.

"You did okay, you know," she said after a period of quiet consideration.

He met her gaze again, knowing he'd regret it but unable to resist. "If you mean I got over it, you're right."

She shook her head, sending a tendril of pure auburn silk curling against her cheek. "I'm not sure we ever get over things like that, but you didn't let it make you bitter. Not really."

Not really? Now, what was that supposed to mean?

Before he could demand clarification, she added, "You steer away from commitment, but from everything I can see, you've made it your life's work to keep that kind of hurt from happening to anyone else under your watch. You turned what could have been bitterness into something constructive. That's special." She smiled and shook her head. "And all this time I thought you were just some shallow chump who had nothing but sex on his brain."

He feared she might have been more right than she knew. "I'll take that as a compliment."

"Good." She sipped her coffee, then set the cup carefully on a coaster. "It is a compliment. You're one of the good guys. A white knight. You should be proud of what you do."

If she had targeted his ego, she'd hit the mark. That she thought so highly of his work meant a great deal more to him than it should have. "While we're confessing," he offered, feeling the need to show his appreciation somehow, "I have to admit you're definitely not what I expected on a professional level, either."

She held up both hands. "You don't have to tell me that you thought I was taking advantage of Alexandra. You've already made that quite clear."

He placed his own mug on the table and leaned forward, bracing his elbows on his knees. "No, I'm serious. You really are good with children. Alexandra is lucky to have you on her staff." Their gazes connected, his firm, hers startled. "And as a sister."

The new glimmer of emotion that flickered in her eyes tightened his gut, made him want to reach across the table and touch her. But that would only lead them right back to what they'd scarcely escaped last night.

"That means a lot." She turned her attention to Chris. "I'm glad we had this time together."

Keith tried to decipher what he'd seen in her eyes and what he'd heard in her voice just then, but couldn't. The only thing he knew for certain was that they'd ventured into dangerous territory again. Already something inside him felt raw and exposed. What was it about this woman that could make him want things he'd never wanted before?

A knock at the door kept him from having to dredge up the answers to that question—an answer he probably wouldn't like.

He frowned as he went to the door. Had Jaron returned with news of next of kin? That would be the best possible thing. Then why did it feel the exact opposite? Keith mentally kicked himself for even going down that path.

When he opened the door he found Annabelle standing on the deck, looking more than a little uncertain.

"ANNABELLE?" Shana pushed past Keith and joined her friend outside. "Why are you here?" She noticed Harold sniffing around the yard and couldn't help smiling. "I mean, has something happened? Is there news?"

Annabelle shrugged. "A hunch."

"Come on in," Keith suggested. "There's coffee and muffins."

She offered him a strained smile. "In a minute."

Obviously taking that as a cue to give the women some space, Keith ducked back inside, leaving them alone for a moment.

"What sort of hunch?" Shana prodded. She kept remembering what Keith had said about Jaron suspecting that Annabelle was hiding something.

"I'm not really sure." Annabelle looked sorely uncomfortable. "Can I see her again?"

"Well, of course you can." Shana gestured toward the door, which still stood wide open in invitation. "Come on in."

Annabelle shook her head as she moved forward. "I'm probably imagining things."

As soon as they were inside, Annabelle moved over to the sofa to look at the baby. "Thank heaven I didn't tell Jaron," she murmured, more to herself than to Shana.

Shana was really worried now. She glanced toward the kitchen, where Keith had his back turned and was loading the dishwasher.

"What didn't you tell Jaron?" Shana asked quietly, easing down on the coffee table so she would be eye level with Annabelle, who'd taken a seat on the sofa next to Chris.

Annabelle glanced in Keith's direction. He was now wiping down the counters. "He's quite domestic, isn't he?" she remarked offhandedly. She directed an obviously fake smile toward Shana. "Lucky you."

Something was very wrong. Shana could sense the tension in her friend. "Tell Jaron what?" she urged again, hoping to get to the bottom of the problem and avoid any discussion of Keith.

Emotion shone in Annabelle's eyes as she twisted her hands together in her lap. "I've been stupid."

"You want to tell us why?" Keith asked gently as he came up beside the table where Shana sat.

Annabelle's gaze flicked from him to the baby

sleeping in the makeshift cradle. "I just..." She frowned. "I thought the couple who died...they're fine-boned and lean. And this little one...well, she's round-faced and chubby. I don't know. It was just a momentary impression." She shook her head. "It was nothing, I suppose."

"I was round-faced and chubby," Keith interjected. "Michelin man." He laughed, but it sounded put on. "Or Michelin baby—that was me. I think I was born with three spare tires." He rolled up his sleeve and flexed his arm. "But look at me now," he mused with a slight grin. "Pure muscle."

Shana had to laugh, though she was certain this was no laughing matter. "I think maybe you'd better stick to the kitchen chores."

"I believe I've just been insulted," he said petulantly. Even Annabelle managed a laugh at his indignant look.

They lapsed into silence for a while, but Shana's thoughts were racing with possibilities. God, what if Jaron was right and Annabelle was hiding something?

"Annabelle," Keith said kindly, "we're all upset over this. We're worried about what will happen to the baby. But you can't read anything into a baby's parentage by the way she looks at four weeks old. Or not much, anyway."

Annabelle still seemed unconvinced. "I know."

Shana eased to the edge of the table. There was something here. She could sense it. "What are you thinking?" She watched the indecision and doubt shadow Annabelle's face.

"I'm not sure."

"That the couple who died weren't the baby's parents?" Keith's expression had gone deadly serious. "I thought you said there was evidence that the woman had given birth recently."

"There is. She had."

"So…" Keith allowed the single word to hang in the air.

Annabelle sat up a little straighter and looked him square in the eye. "They were running for a reason. They'd come a long way after stealing the car. The police have found no reports of crimes that would indicate this couple as suspects. But there had to be something that sent them fleeing."

"It's early in the investigation yet," Keith countered. "These things take time."

The doctor shook her head. "I know it sounds stupid. It was just… I looked at the photographs I'd taken and she seemed so chubby, so different from the couple. But you're right." She stared down at the sleeping infant once more. "Looking at her now…" She shrugged again and sighed. "There's no reason to doubt her parentage, I guess."

Keith and Shana exchanged a look. She knew what he was thinking before he spoke. "It would definitely complicate matters if the child wasn't a biological match with the couple."

"That's why you're here," Shana said suddenly. A shiver of fear swept over her. "You're not sure. You had to have another look."

"I..." Annabelle didn't bother denying what Shana could clearly see in her eyes.

"Just tell us what you need, Annabelle," Keith urged. "We're your friends. You can tell us."

"I thought perhaps a blood test would be in order." She was wringing her hands again. "Nothing complicated like DNA profiling, just a simple blood test."

"You know that's not always conclusive," Keith said evenly.

"That's true." Annabelle leveled a gaze on him that sent a feeling of dread through Shana once more. "But if they're not compatible..."

"Geezus, you really think you're on to something, don't you?" Keith had paled.

"I didn't say that," Annabelle insisted defensively. She stood, matching his stance. "But having thought it, having wondered...well, what would it hurt? Maybe I should do the test and find out."

IT TOOK SHANA ALMOST an hour to get the baby settled after Annabelle's visit. Keith didn't think it was the blood sample Annabelle had withdrawn as much as her very presence that upset the child.

Shana had put the idea in his head and it had stuck. What if the baby recognized the doctor's voice and was disturbed by the memories it evoked? Keith couldn't help thinking the whole idea was ridiculous, but still...

This entire case was growing more and more confusing. Annabelle's behavior today had made him uneasy.

"She's down for the count, I think," Shana said as she rejoined him in the great room. She'd tucked the baby into bed upstairs so that their talking wouldn't disturb her. The door was open in case she woke up and cried out for their attention.

"Something's wrong here," he said. He stood behind a chair, bracing his hands on its back. "I've never seen Annabelle so unsure of herself."

Shana curled up at one end of the couch. Keith's intense concentration was momentarily distracted by how much at home she looked on his sofa. He pushed the idea away.

"I noticed her behaving oddly yesterday when we took the photographs," Shana told him. "She seemed so nervous…so worried about what might happen next."

Annabelle hadn't been the only one behaving strangely during that photo shoot, but Keith wasn't about to bring up his own ridiculous performance.

But there had been one thing…. "Maybe there's something going on between her and Jaron," he said almost to himself. "Jaron acted a little oddly himself."

When his eyes met Shana's, Keith knew what she was thinking. This whole thing seemed to be getting to everyone, including the two of them. Maybe Annabelle and Jaron were suffering from the same proximity disorder that plagued Shana and him.

"What if she's right?"

Shana's fearful words tugged him back to the matter at hand. "She's only speculating," he assured her.

Shana worried her lower lip with her teeth, setting Keith instantly on edge, making him want to soothe that tortured flesh with his tongue. He shook himself and ordered his brain to focus.

"I just can't do this." Shana pushed up from the sofa and started to pace. "I can't…it's too much."

There was no way to make any of this right. She knew it and so did he. But he had to try—for the baby and for her. "We'll do everything we can. She'll be safe—"

Shana turned on him. "But will she be loved?" She moved closer, taking his breath away with the intensity of the emotions reflected in her eyes. "Will they treat her like their own? Can you promise me that?"

"I can't—"

She shook her head, cutting off his words. "I knew you couldn't." She poked him in the chest with her forefinger. "You'll let Child Services take her away and you'll have no say in the matter of who ultimately takes care of her. It'll be the luck of the draw."

She was going to cry. She blinked furiously to stop the tears, but they spilled past her lashes anyway, making her angrier and tying his gut into a thousand knots.

"I'll do everything I can," he insisted. But she was right. Once Child Services took over, it would be out of his hands. He'd been fooling himself to think otherwise. He couldn't make sure little Chrissy was safe and happy. He could only do what the law allowed.

"Please, Keith," Shana begged. "Don't let them

take her away. If Annabelle is right, there's no telling how long this could go on." She swiped at her cheeks with the backs of her hands and peered up at him with those huge brown eyes. "I don't want her to be in limbo that long. She doesn't need any more strangers thrust into her life."

He couldn't deny himself any longer...he had to touch Shana. He took her by the arms, but restrained himself from pulling her closer. "What is it you're asking, Shana? What do you expect me to do?"

"Let me take care of her. You know I will. Don't turn her over to strangers. She's already been through enough."

God, how he wished he could do that. "You know I can't allow it. The law—"

"Then we'll keep her together." Her chin came up, challenge replacing the softer emotions in her eyes. "We've made it through the weekend. We can do it."

If she only knew how tempted he was! But that arrangement would cause them both trouble in the end. It would lead to places neither of them wanted to go. "You don't mean that."

"Yes, I do." She grabbed his shirt in a fist and moved closer, daringly so. "We'll play this any way you want, as long as the baby stays with us until this case is solved and whatever family she has is found."

She was offering him what he'd told her he wanted.

His heart stumbled once, twice.

She was willing to go against her own rules for the welfare of the baby.

What kind of monster did she think he was? Hadn't

she just told him this morning that she'd been wrong about him?

"Do you really think I'd let you do that?" He studied her closely, hoping to find some glimmer of doubt in her eyes.

She blinked away whatever he thought he saw. "All I'm saying is that we can do this."

She doubted him that much. That realization hurt more than it should have. Had her opinion of him come to mean so much to him, or was his ego simply bruised?

Uncertainty thundering in his brain, he wrapped his fingers around her wrists and pulled her hands free of his shirt. "If you're sure you're prepared to make this kind of time commitment, then so am I."

Her expression was suffused with gratitude. "I'm sure."

Tears welled once more, and he was confident he couldn't bear to see them fall again. "We'll stay here for a few days until we've taken care of the logistics, then we can move to my town house in the city. If that's acceptable to you."

She nodded eagerly. "That's fine. My apartment is so small, and there's only one bed—"

She caught herself then, her cheeks flaming scarlet.

"You're right," he agreed. "My place has two bedrooms. We'll be most comfortable there."

For just one second he thought he saw disappointment flash in her eyes, but it vanished so quickly he couldn't be sure.

"You'd really do this for the baby?" she asked.

Her face was wiped clean of emotion, but her voice held a telltale note of wonder. She couldn't believe he would commit like this without recompense. She didn't have to say it outright. He could read between the lines.

"Yes, I'll do it for the baby." He snagged her hand when she would have turned away, apparently satisfied with his answer. But it wasn't enough for him. She had to know the rest—the part he'd only just realized himself. When her gaze connected fully with his once more, he told her, "And I'll do it for you."

She searched his eyes, one second turning into five, before she asked, "Why would you do that for me? We don't even like each other, remember?"

She was right. Until a couple of days ago they'd been at each other's throats each time they passed in the hospital corridors. He had no definitive answer for her. He wasn't sure she would want to hear what he did have to say. But it was the truth, and somehow he sensed that, for them, truth was of the utmost importance.

"Because I don't want to be another one of those people you counted on who let you down."

CHAPTER ELEVEN

SHANA PEERED OUT the window, watching Keith as he strolled leisurely around the front of the property. She couldn't be sure if he was really so interested in the trees bordering the yard or if he'd just needed to escape the confines of the cabin. She'd considered escaping herself, but he'd beat her to the punch.

After his profound announcement this morning that he had no intention of letting her down as others in her life had, he'd mumbled something about needing a walk, and had wasted no time in getting out the door.

Now she was thoroughly confused.

She hugged her arms around herself and sighed. Just when she thought she had the guy figured out, he went and did something totally unexpected.

Yes, she'd already seen through that slick, charming exterior and recognized that he cared greatly about his job and the people whose interests he represented. She also fully understood that his need to conceal the depth of his compassion was an attempt to fend off deeper relationships.

He wasn't about to risk his heart to anyone.

The very idea of having children scared him to

death. That frightened little boy who lived deep inside him wanted to protect others from the horrifying experiences he'd endured.

And all that only made her want him, made her care for him, more.

Closing her eyes, Shana exhaled in utter defeat. She was hopeless. She'd fallen for the guy, hook, line and sinker. And it had nothing to do with fishing. Not that she would soon forget their lovely outing to the creek and the fact that he'd tossed back every single fish he'd caught just to please her.

She hadn't been fishing for Keith Hewitt. She hadn't even liked him.

Or had she?

Denial raced through her. Maybe beneath the surface…

But agreeing to share the weekend with him had been about the baby. She glanced at the upstairs landing. Little Chris still slept soundly. Shana had wanted to protect the baby just as much as Keith had, though he'd come to the realization more slowly. Her every intuition told her that he was accustomed to hiding his true feelings, to denying them, actually. He'd done a pretty darn good job of fooling himself into believing that he didn't want or need commitment.

That was something a lot of men did. Take her brother, for example. He always hid his true feelings, even when their mother had passed away. He'd never let his hurt show, not once. And when it had come to meeting Alexandra Webber, he'd flatly refused. He wanted nothing to do with more family. In his opinion, Shana was the only family he had.

Despite his pigheadedness, she missed him immensely.

She glanced at the telephone. She should call him.

Before the thought fully meshed in her head, she was at the telephone entering the number.

Brett answered on the second ring. "Yeah."

"It's me."

A heavy breath hissed across the line.

"I love you, too," Shana said pointedly.

"You know I'm always glad to hear from you, sis," he grumped. "As long as you're not planning to try and talk me into coming out to Seattle, that is."

"I do miss you," she admitted, "but I respect your feelings, even if I don't agree with them."

A beat of silence echoed before he responded. "I miss you, too."

A smile slid over her lips. Every once in a while a little emotion slipped past his defenses. "You been working hard?"

"Taking a break between cases," he allowed. Brett never discussed his work in-depth with her. A private investigator, he insisted that confidentiality prevented him from disclosing the nature of his assignments. She respected that, too, but she still worried.

"You could come see me," she ventured, knowing full well that was exactly what he didn't want to hear. "Just for a day," she interjected quickly. "Only me, no one else."

"I don't have that kind of time."

Irritation knitted her brows. "I thought you said you were taking a break."

He gave another mighty exhalation. "Could we not go down this road? Please?" he added when she remained silent.

What was the point in pursuing the issue? Shana thought. She wasn't going to change his mind. Her headstrong brother would have to come to his own conclusions in his own time.

"Sorry," she said, relenting. "So how are things?"

He chuckled softly. "Things are fine. And you?"

She plopped onto the couch, her mood lifting slightly. "Oh, I'm okay, I guess."

There was another little stretch of silence.

Shana realized her mistake instantly.

"What's going on, sis?"

Too late.

With those five little words she'd uttered, he'd read her like a book. They'd always been that close—close enough to recognize from the slightest nuance in tone that something was off-kilter.

"Nothing." Shana replied too quickly. "Why do you think something is going on? I swear, you've been in the P.I. business too long. You're always trying to read between the lines." She picked imaginary lint from her sweater to distract herself.

"I was your brother a long time before becoming a P.I. Now, what's up?"

Shana exhaled a disgusted sigh. "I've met someone," she confessed, knowing he wouldn't shut up until she spilled her news. Brett should be an interrogator for the FBI. He was relentless.

"Someone?"

There was no way to miss the skepticism in his voice, which annoyed her all the more. "Yes," she snapped. "Someone."

"Look, Shana," he said in that knowing tone that warned her a counseling session would surely follow, "we both have a problem with relationships. Don't go getting yourself hurt."

"I don't have a problem with relationships." Every time they talked about their social lives, they ended up at this sore point.

"You can't have had an overbearing, suspicious mother like ours and still trust. You know that. Why pretend? It's the way it is. We both know we can't count on anyone but ourselves."

"But this guy's different. He…he could be the one." Her breath stalled in her lungs. Had she really said that? She couldn't be sure Keith was different, but something made her want to believe he was.

"Yeah, right. You would be an expert in that department. How many relationships have you had? Two? No, maybe it's one. How well do you know this guy? When did you meet him?"

Anger seethed, and unfortunately, she wasn't successful at keeping it out of her voice. She darn sure wasn't going to tell him she'd only really known Keith for the weekend. "He *is* different. He's like us. He's been let down in the past and knows how it feels."

Brett laughed. "And that's supposed to make him different? You think that because he's been there, you can trust him? That only makes him more likely to cut and run."

Enough. She wasn't going to argue about trust with a guy who clearly had none. "Just forget I said anything." She shook her head and mentally kicked herself for mentioning Keith.

"Look," Brett said with a sigh, "I just don't want you to get hurt. I know how badly you want that whole Ozzie and Harriet thing, but you gotta get real, sis. The chances of finding that fantasy are just about nil. All that true-love stuff is pretty much crap. It comes along maybe once in a lifetime—so how the hell are you supposed to recognize the right one? Why even take the risk?"

God, she hated to accept that life had done this to both of them, leaving them afraid to trust, afraid to take a chance.

"But if we don't risk it," she said, voicing the thought, "how will we ever know?"

The heavy cloak of silence thickened between them for a long while before Brett said what the two of them had felt for far too long. "Maybe it's best if we don't."

They both made a conscious effort to avoid the subject for the rest of the conversation. Brett was determined not to be hurt by anyone—as Keith was. Shana couldn't help wondering how she'd managed to fall for a guy so very much like the brother she loved so dearly.

But Brett was right about one thing—she wanted the fantasy. That was true. She'd lied to herself long enough. She wanted a husband, one who would love and cherish her for the rest of her life. Who would never let her down.

And maybe her brother was right about another thing: maybe there was no such man. Shana returned to the window, where her searching gaze sought and found Keith once more. But if she never took the chance…

She had to know, had to take the risk.

Her heartbeat picked up in pace. This was the first time in a very long time that she'd wanted to trust her heart to someone. She couldn't be that wrong about Keith. It was time she trusted not only him, but herself.

That was the real bottom line. She had to trust herself before she ever trusted anyone else. It was past time she learned to do that.

SHANA STOOD NEAR the front door clutching her purse when Keith finally returned to the cabin. He'd taken a long walk around the property and tried to reason out his thoughts, hoping to regain some perspective. He'd thought he'd accomplished that, until he came face-to-face with Shana once more.

He still wanted her. Wanted her desperately. And not just to make love to her. He also wanted to protect her, to make sure no one ever hurt her again.

This was insane. They barely knew each other.

And yet those feelings were stronger than any he'd ever experienced.

"I need to go back into the city," she said, jerking him from his troubling thoughts.

He blinked. So that's why she was holding her purse.

A cold hard fist of fear slammed into his gut.

She'd changed her mind.

"Why?" He tried to keep the fear out of his voice, but failed miserably. "We're going back tomorrow."

She forced a smile. He'd seen the real McCoy and knew this was not it. "Well," she said nervously, "Chris needs diapers, since we didn't get around to picking up any, and it would probably be good to get more formula and a couple more changes of clothes for her." She moistened those full lips, and desire shuddered through him. It took every ounce of strength he possessed not to reach out and touch her. "I'll need to talk to someone about changing to day shift temporarily. I can take Chris to work with me and then be with her at night, as well. And I thought I'd go by my apartment and pick up a few things, since we've decided to…decided to stay here a while longer."

She hadn't changed her mind.

Relief made him weak. "Of course," he croaked, then gestured to the table where his keys lay. "You'll probably need to get gas before you get on the interstate."

She nodded, snagged his keys and then plastered

on another of those fake smiles. "The baby's still sleeping. I'll make it quick."

Shana rushed out the door without looking back. Keith watched her drive away, still wondering if she'd change her mind.

No, he felt certain she wouldn't walk out on little Chris like that. Now, walking out on him was a whole other matter. That she might do...not that he could blame her.

Hell, he wasn't even sure he wouldn't want to run himself before this was over. But for the first time in his life, he had every intention of seeing it through.

If anyone walked out it would be Shana. Not him. He'd given his word that he wouldn't let her down, and he wouldn't.

No matter what it cost him.

SHANA STOOD OUTSIDE the door to Annabelle's apartment for a long while before she knocked. She'd already stopped at the supercenter and gotten the diapers, formula and other necessities she and the baby would need for a longer stay at the cabin. She'd checked her own answering machine for calls and made the necessary change to her work schedule with a co-worker. Then she'd packed a week's wardrobe and lugged the bags down to Keith's SUV. She hadn't thought to bring her suitcases from the cabin, so she'd had to use shopping bags. She could have gotten her clothes tomorrow, but she was buying time. She needed to be away from Keith just a little while longer. There were no more excuses left, however.

Still, before she could leave, she had to see Annabelle. Shana had to know if there was any news, and if Annabelle had done the blood test. That would give her a few more minutes.

Taking a deep, bolstering breath, Shana raised her fist and rapped on the door. It opened before she could knock a second time. Annabelle stared bleary-eyed at Shana, a tissue clutched in her hand.

"Hi." Shana mustered a smile to mask her concern.

"Shana?" Annabelle visibly scrambled to pull herself together. "Why aren't you up at the cabin?"

"We needed diapers," she said with false cheer, then shrugged. "And I thought one of us should find out what was going on. May I come in?"

Confusion joined the emotions on Annabelle's flushed face. "Of course." She backed up and held the door open for Shana to come inside, then closed it behind her. "But aren't you returning to town tonight, anyway?" she asked as she moved across the room and settled behind her desk.

Shana sighed and slumped into the chair flanking the desk. She might as well confess all. Annabelle would likely see through her attempts to hide the truth. "We'll be coming down tomorrow morning to work and to sort things out." She shrugged again. "We still have to finalize the details." Her gaze connected with her friend's. "We thought we might stay up at the cabin for a little while longer. To take care of the baby until next of kin is found," she added quickly.

Annabelle's keen powers of perception shone right through her misery. "Shana—"

"Don't ask any questions," she pleaded wearily, wringing her hands, "because I can't answer them. Not yet. Right now I'm too confused. I only know that things are happening that I don't really understand, but I'm going to give them every chance of working out." She searched Annabelle's eyes, hoping to find understanding. "I have to."

"You and Keith...?"

"Haven't slept together," she replied in answer to the unspoken question. "Not yet, anyway." Annabelle glanced away, leaving Shana confused.

"You look like hell, by the way," she commented, drawing the doctor's attention back to her, but diverting it from the subject of Keith...she hoped.

"Gee, thanks," Annabelle said dryly.

"Don't mention it. What are friends for?" At least if they were talking about Annabelle's situation, they wouldn't be discussing Shana's.

"To boost my spirits?" Annabelle countered. "To tell me watery is the newest look in makeup?"

"Watery isn't a look I would associate with you." Shana could attest to that without reservation. Annabelle was the strongest woman she knew.

"Why not?" The question went way beyond defensive; anger flared in Annabelle's expression. "When I'm cut, I bleed."

"Like the rest of the human race?" Shana didn't want to hurt her friend, but honesty was far more important right now than anything else. This was no time for flowery words or white lies, even if the truth kindled her anger.

"Yes." The single word was cold, hard.

"You don't usually admit that the human race has anything to do with you...or vice versa," Shana said carefully, not wanting to hurt her unnecessarily.

"So..." Annabelle's mouth worked as she struggled to find the proper words. She looked every bit as confused as Shana felt.

Shana knew that look, knew it well. The doctor had it as bad as she did...or maybe worse.

"It's Jaron, isn't it?"

Annabelle's gaze speared hers. "It's the baby," she countered.

Shana shook her head slowly as comprehension dawned. "I saw the way you were with each other yesterday. It's definitely Jaron." Her heart went out to her friend. "Oh, Annabelle."

Annabelle sniffed and glowered at her. "Oh Annabelle, nothing!"

Shana knew all too well exactly how she felt. "Definitely something. Have you slept with him?"

Annabelle didn't have to speak. The answer was written all over her face. Despite what Shana had suspected, she felt surprise as she sat farther back in her chair. "Oh, my God. You have!" She thought of everything Keith had told her about Jaron. "He probably hasn't been with a woman since his wife was killed." Her gaze collided with Annabelle's once more, and the answer to the next question was right there in her eyes. "Have you even dated anyone since coming here?'' Not once since Shana hired on at the hospital had she heard even the vaguest hint of gossip regarding Annabelle's social life. It was like her own—nonexistent.

''It's none of your business.''

True, but Shana had a feeling the whole thing went deeper than that. She suddenly wondered if Annabelle had ever slept with anyone, period. Not that Shana could cite much experience herself, but...

Time for a subject change.

Annabelle was right, this wasn't any of her business.

''Tell me what's happening with the baby,'' Shana suggested softly, hoping to ease the tension. ''What did the blood test tell you?''

For a moment, Annabelle simply looked at her, as if the news was too unbelievable to put into words. Finally she said, ''That the couple killed weren't her biological parents.''

Shana was the one who couldn't speak this time. How could that be true? Was Annabelle sure? Was this what Jaron had suspected all along?

''Whoa,'' she managed to say eventually. ''Does Seth know?'' He would have a stroke. If this got out...

''Not yet.''

Dear God, had she told anyone? ''And Jaron?''

''I've told him.''

Relief washed over Shana, then comprehension. ''Which is why you're so soggy.'' Annabelle must have had a meeting with him shortly before Shana's arrival.

"Shana—"

She held up her hands, palms out. "Hey, I know I'm making assumptions here, but I'm right, aren't I?"

Annabelle lost the battle with the emotions churning inside her. The struggle played out on every delicate feature of her face. "He thinks I'm such a loser. I should have told him before. I could have said…"

Her words trailed off, but Shana had to know if Jaron's suspicions had been right all along. Surely Annabelle hadn't kept this kind of secret. "Said what?"

Annabelle's gaze locked with hers. "That I knew something was wrong right from the start…almost. The woman…she didn't even want to look at the baby when I held her close to her." She shook her head, a frown marring her brow. "She'd call out for her baby and then ignore her. It didn't make sense."

Shana remained quiet, too stunned to respond, and certain on some level that she needed to allow Annabelle to tell the story at her own pace.

"She looked right through the baby, sobbing in fear for her child, when we were telling her over and over that the baby was fine and right there next to her. She didn't seem to hear us." She chewed her lower lip a moment. "And then…"

Her silence dragged on until Shana couldn't take it any longer. "And then?" she prodded.

"She told me that he made her do it. She kept

wailing that her baby was going to die, and then she'd beg me to find her and help her. Then she made me promise that I'd tell no one.'' Annabelle closed her eyes as if the memories flooding back were nearly more than she could bear. ''She was so afraid of her husband.'' Her gaze settled on Shana once more. ''He made her do it. I know he did. The woman's fear was real. She only wanted to be sure her baby was safe. She'd definitely given birth approximately one month ago, but not to Chris.''

''God.'' It was all Shana could think to say.

''I didn't connect everything at first,'' Annabelle murmured, still caught up in the memories. ''But I promised I wouldn't tell. I wanted to protect her....'' She looked directly into Shana's eyes. ''It was past time someone had.''

And then Shana knew. Annabelle was feeling guilty that she hadn't told Jaron everything from the start.

''I think maybe I would have done the same thing,'' Shana said. And it was true. Who could say? The woman had been dying. It was her last wish....

''You would?''

She sat up straighter. ''You found out the car was stolen. That was enough to explain the 'my husband made me do it' remark. There wasn't anything in that to indicate something as awful as a stolen baby.''

''But—''

''But,'' Shana interrupted, ''she was dying. She was practically incoherent. You couldn't have expected this sort of thing, and the moment you even vaguely wondered, you took steps to check. I think you've done the right thing, and if you'd like, I'll say so to Jaron.''

Annabelle huffed in disbelief. ''I don't think he'll listen.''

''Then he's a fool.'' Shana pushed herself out of her chair and moved around the desk to crouch next to her friend. She took Annabelle's hand in hers. ''You're a very nice person, Annabelle Peters. I don't know what you're running from or why you're holding yourself back from the human race, but I do know that you've got integrity and courage, and you care. None of this is your fault.''

Annabelle tried to pull away, but Shana held on. ''You need a friend here,'' she added gently. ''You need someone to take you out and buy you amaretto and ice cream and chocolate-filled Oreos. In bulk.''

''I do not need—''

''Yes you do.'' Shana squeezed her hand. ''Let me be that friend. I could use some ice cream and Oreos myself.'' They were both fighting the same battle—trust. It was so damn hard to trust when you'd been let down so many times in your life. But she and Annabelle had to stand tall now and suck it up. The chance at true love—at real trust—didn't come around often. They had to take the risk. Jaron Dorsey was a good man. Shana knew his reputation even if she didn't really know him.

Annabelle almost smiled. ''And what about Keith?''

A little smile of her own peeked out when his name

was mentioned. "Keith can wait." Shana stood and drew her friend to her feet. "Let's go find that comfort food."

Still a tad reluctant, Annabelle allowed Shana to drag her from the apartment she used more often than not to hide away in. Shana was sincerely looking forward to some female bonding time.

She just hoped she was right about Keith.

He might not like being made to wait, no matter how good the excuse.

She could only pray that he would understand and be patient, and that he wouldn't change his mind about the proposition he'd made that they take care of the baby together.

Shana also prayed that she hadn't misconstrued what she assumed to be his proposition—that he wanted to get to know her better. She could call, but a part of her wanted to see how he would measure up to this little test.

She just wasn't sure her heart could take that kind of letdown if he didn't. But whatever the risk, she was willing to take it. Every fiber of her being told her that Keith Hewitt, despite all she'd once thought about him, was well worth taking a chance on.

CHAPTER TWELVE

THE AFTERNOON SUN HAD settled behind the trees for the evening and still Shana hadn't returned.

"She'll be back," he muttered to himself, or maybe to the baby resting against his shoulder.

Little Chris had wailed like a banshee when she first awoke after Shana left for the city. Keith had quickly figured out that she'd slept so long she was simply ravenous and needed her bottle. He'd managed that task, and then he'd burped her and wrestled a fresh diaper onto her tiny bottom.

He patted the infernal thing now and wondered what idiot had come up with the design. The tapes never stayed in place and the smallest size was entirely too large for a newborn.

But in the end, she was fed and dry. And now she slept again. That was another thing he'd learned about newborns in the past couple of days: they slept a lot. When they weren't sleeping, they were generally doing one of two things, eating or crying. He supposed crying was their only means of communication. He shifted Chris into his arms and smiled down at her. The thing was, babies were just so darn cute.

His stomach tightened and he had the nearly overpowering desire to hold a child of his own. That revelation startled him so much he had to swallow back the lump in his throat. Not once in his life had he longed for fatherhood as much as he did now. He forced back the unfamiliar feeling. This was not a good sign.

It was Shana. She had him pondering all sorts of crazy notions. In spite of his anxiety, he smiled and shook his head. It was official now. He'd definitely lost all control over his emotions and any grip on rational thought. He wanted to risk a relationship with the woman who had been the bane of his existence more than he wanted to take his next breath.

The whole notion made absolutely no sense, and threatened his heart as well as his reputation as a confirmed bachelor.

But he had to try. Had to know if he could fall in love with Shana the way he longed to.

Love. He shook his head again and slowly climbed the stairs. What did he know about it? He'd loved his parents, certainly. If he'd known either set of his grandparents, he'd have no doubt loved them. He'd had relationships where he'd grown fond of his female companion, but he'd never been in love with anyone. Maybe he didn't know how to fall in love. Hell, he wasn't even certain actual effort was involved. Perhaps it happened all on its own. But how would he know?

The image of Shana filled his mind; the remembered taste of her tingled on his lips. And just like that, he was certain he could figure it out. All he had to do was keep his head on straight and take it slow. He felt relatively confident that neither of them wanted to rush into anything. Taking things slowly was imperative, especially for two people who had so much trouble with trust.

One step at a time, one moment at a time, was the way to go about this. No jumping into anything. Like bed. His gaze settled on the wide bed where she'd slept the last three nights.

"Now, that's a first," he muttered as he tucked the sleeping baby into her makeshift cradle.

His entire adult life he had enjoyed sex tremendously. Had considered it above all else when it came to his social life. He hadn't been interested in commitment, so what else was there? Just the sex. And he'd liked it that way.

But sex with Shana felt secondary to something else—something he couldn't quite name. But he could feel its pull. He wanted to be close to her, to touch her, but he wanted more than to simply have sex with her.

He wanted to make love to her...long, slow and languid.

Releasing a heavy breath, he eased out of the room. This was too damn surreal. He'd never once felt like this—so confused yet so determined.

Trudging down the stairs, feeling utterly at a loss and at the same time resigned to his fate, he couldn't help wondering if maybe she'd changed her mind.

She hadn't come back, after all.

He peered out the window into the darkening

gloom. Maybe she'd decided she didn't want to risk this kind of relationship. Not that either of them had put a plan into words, other than for the baby, but they both knew what was really at stake here on a personal level. A relationship. Seeing only each other. Spending all their time outside work together. Getting to know one another on many levels.

Having a physical union.

That last thought sent blood rushing to his groin. Just thinking about having her made him hard, and she wasn't even in the room. Hell, she wasn't even in the vicinity. Desperate to know that she was okay, he phoned her apartment. When the answering machine picked up, he disconnected. Surely she was on her way by now.

Forcing his attention to dinner, he went to the kitchen and surveyed the possibilities. Soup and salad, he decided. Since he wasn't sure what time she would return, the soup would be easy to warm up.

And he was certain she would be back.

If not for him, for the baby.

His chest constricted and he battled the disturbing thoughts from his mind. That was the thing about trust. One had to actually put it into practice. There was no time like the present.

He trusted that Shana would come back…to him.

DARKNESS HAD FALLEN when Shana parked the SUV in front of the cabin. It had taken some time to perk up Annabelle, not to mention to consume numerous helpings of high-calorie ice cream and all the trimmings. Almost groaning with discomfort, Shana patted her tummy and wondered if she'd ever want ice cream again.

But all that mattered was that her friend's depression had lifted considerably. Of course, Shana had left her with a little something other than ice cream to get her through the night. Had almost considered having a drink or two herself, except that she'd known she had to drive back here.

Truth was, Shana admitted as she sat there in the vehicle long after she'd parked, she had been putting off this very moment. She looked up at the cabin and noted that every light downstairs was on. Keith was waiting for her. She wondered vaguely if the baby had given him a hard time, but mostly she wondered if he'd missed her. If he'd changed his mind and decided against pursuing whatever this was between them.

Shana closed her eyes and released a shaky breath. "Please don't let this be a mistake," she prayed.

When she opened her eyes, she couldn't help smiling. Keith was on the deck. Her heart did a funny little acrobatic routine and then took off in a flat-out run.

Pushing open the driver's-side door, she scooted out of the seat just as he strolled up to the vehicle.

"Need some help with that?" He nodded toward the back seat and the bags of clothing and newly purchased goods.

Even in the car's dim interior lighting, she could

see the uncertainty on his face. She wasn't the only one worried here. Somehow that gave her courage.

"Help would be nice."

Lapsing into a comfortable silence, they hauled the load of goods into the cabin and stored everything appropriately. Several trips were required to accomplish the task, but neither of them was in a hurry. To pass the time, she told him about the blood test and the development between Annabelle and Jaron.

With every moment that passed and every step they took, her heart beat just a little faster. It felt good walking alongside Keith. Shana wanted to be held in his arms…to sleep in his arms.

By the time the job was finished, she was pretty sure that something had to give. The sexual tension simmering between them had grown to unbearable proportions. She was certain Keith felt it, too.

"I can warm up dinner if you're hungry," he offered when they descended the stairs after taking the last of Shana's belongings to her room.

Oh, she was hungry all right but it had nothing to do with food. "You know," she said, moving back toward the stairs, "I think I'll take a shower."

"Maybe later, then," he offered, looking anywhere but at her.

And that was good, Shana decided, because she was pretty sure she would never have been able to climb those steps if he'd given her just the right look of invitation. At least she wouldn't have been climbing them alone.

She warned herself again to take it slow. The last

thing they needed was to be in a hurry. This had to be done the right way. It was far too important to rush.

Shana hurried into the en suite bath and twisted the faucet, sending water spraying from the showerhead. *Slow and easy,* she told herself. That was what they both needed. But restraint was proving far more difficult than she'd anticipated.

If she made it through this night without throwing herself at his feet, she'd be damn lucky.

HE WASN'T GOING TO survive this.

Keith placed the salad and plates on the island counter, arranging and rearranging them until he finally just had to walk away.

All he could think about was that she'd come back, prepared to stay at least a week.

That was what he wanted, wasn't it?

Of course it was.

He just wasn't sure where to go from here.

Should they talk some more? Share family photo albums and old stories? Or should they chuck it all and do what he knew for a fact they both wanted?

He placed the covered serving bowl of soup in the microwave and set it on medium power for the appropriate number of minutes. He had to eat whether she did or not.

It was either eat or go to bed. He couldn't bear another waking minute without occupying himself somehow.

Just as the microwave dinged, Shana descended the stairs.

Every good intention he possessed vanished instantly at the sight of her in a big fluffy robe that covered nearly every inch of her. Her auburn hair was still wet and clinging to her neck, the only part of her besides her face that wasn't covered in white terry cloth. The need to touch her exploded inside him, making him tremble.

"Hungry now?" His voice was rough with a desire he couldn't disguise. He cleared his throat, knowing full well that wouldn't change a damn thing.

She smiled as she moved down the final step. "Starved."

Her eyes glittered with something that looked very much like sexual hunger—the same hunger he felt— and every muscle in his body reacted.

"Have a seat." He gestured to the nearest chair. "Would you like your salad first?" He had to keep his lust in check. No matter what he thought he saw, he had to be patient. Had to let her make the first move.

Gaining her trust was the first major hurdle, to his way of thinking. Hell, he'd already surrendered his. Not that he'd actually known it until about two seconds ago. But it belonged to her now, to do with as she pleased. For the first time in his adult life, he felt totally helpless and at the mercy of someone else.

"That's fine."

Her salad, he reminded himself, snapping out of the lust-induced trance. A frown creased his brow.

Was it his imagination or was her voice a little huskier than usual? Could she be experiencing the same intensity of desire that he was?

He dismissed the question and picked up their salad plates. *Take it slow,* he told himself. One step at a time. Let her give the first green light.

"Looks yummy," she commented as he set the salad before her.

Keith prided himself in preparing good meals. He considered himself a self-taught master chef. When he was a teenager, learning to cook had been a necessity, since his dad worked. After the long months Keith had spent in foster care, his father had finally been made aware of the situation and had given up his military career. Cooking for the two of them had eventually become a sort of hobby for Keith. He'd even purchased a set of excellent cookbooks. The hobby had turned out to be in his best interests, since he was a bachelor and had to eat.

Focusing on his own plate as he positioned it directly across from Shana, he gave himself a mental pat on the back for keeping his mind off sex. Maybe he could do this, after all.

She stood abruptly, sending her chair clattering to the floor. "I can't keep this up."

Taken aback, he stared down at her, at a loss for words. When he would have slipped around her to rescue her chair, she held up her hands to stop him and shook her head, sending those damp locks of auburn silk dancing around her face. "I promised myself I'd do this right. But I just can't."

Hard as he tried to hold it back, a sigh of defeat whispered past his lips. "I understand." Why had he thought for even a moment that this would work? They had nothing in common except a ferocity where caring for children was concerned. They knew little about each other and had only in the last twenty-four hours been able to inhabit the same room without going for each other's jugular. He should have realized that she would come to her senses, as he should have done. This relationship thing simply wouldn't work.

Ironically, even in the face of her rejection, he still wanted her, a fact that hammered the final nail in the coffin of his stupidity. He was a bigger fool than he had suspected.

She exhaled in what could only be relief. "I'm so glad you understand." She inclined her head in a hint of a shrug and looked sheepish. "I really wanted to try…but I just can't do it."

How many times was she going to say that? Annoyance did little to replace his tightly coiled desire. "Fine. You have to do what you have to do," he offered, letting her off the hook. She didn't have to tell him again that she didn't want him or this…this relationship.

"Great!"

Before he could fathom her next move, she threw her arms around him and kissed him square on the mouth. No timid, careful little kiss, either. This was a blatantly sexual I-want-you-now kind of kiss.

He threw himself into it, kicking aside the last of

his resistance, pitching the whole concept of taking things slowly. She'd made the first move and that's what he'd been waiting for. Why fight it? Her fingers plunged into his hair and she kissed him harder. And he'd thought she wanted out...

He molded his palms to her body, desperate to feel her through all that thick terry cloth. Her fingers trailed down his chest and fumbled with the buttons of his shirt, while his own dived toward her waist and tangled with the knot in the belt holding her robe closed. They had to get out of these clothes, but it was an impossible task with his mind centered on the way her mouth moved beneath his...the way her tongue parlayed with his. She was fire in his arms, her hips moving against his in the most enticing manner.

She shoved his shirt off his shoulders and he released her just long enough to fling it free of his arms. Her robe puddled around her feet, and to his amazement, she stood completely naked before him.

His breath solidified in his lungs. He couldn't move, couldn't speak. He could only look at her.

She was beautiful, exquisitely formed from those voluptuous breasts to her long, shapely legs. Her waist was narrow, her hips slender. Every inch of her was as smooth and creamy as he'd known it would be. And that tempting triangle of curls between her thighs was as auburn and silky looking as the sweet locks he'd run his fingers through over and over.

She moved nearer, reaching for the closure of his trousers. And suddenly he rocketed back into action.

His shoes and trousers went first, then his socks and briefs. She surveyed him with the same thoroughness with which he'd studied her moments before. The approval in her eyes only made him want her more.

He wanted to touch her so very badly, but he waited, allowing her the first move—needing her trust on this level, too. So monumental was the effort of holding back that he trembled with it.

She slipped into his arms, her smooth warm skin caressing his. "I wanted to go at this slowly," she whispered, worry in those beautiful brown eyes.

"Some things just can't be slowed down," he assured her. "It feels right, so it must be right."

A tremulous smile tipped up the corners of her mouth. "It has to be," she agreed.

And then he kissed her with such heart-wrenching tenderness that Shana thought she would go mad. She melted in his arms, the feel of his hard body against hers undoing the last of her reservations. He was as stunning as she'd known he would be, and she wanted him as she'd never wanted anyone before. But in her heart, she knew her desire for him had nothing to do with his physical assets and everything to do with being in love.

Whatever happened from this moment on, she felt certain he was the one. And she would not risk losing out on the one man who made her believe that fantasies really could come true.

He lifted her against him, aligning their hips more closely. The heat and hardness of his body made her whimper with need. His kiss deepened, sending the signal that he was as ready as she was. She wrapped her legs around his waist as he lifted her more fully against him. She needed to feel him nestled against that part of her that longed to be filled by him. A savage groan tore from his throat at her bold move.

He settled her bottom on the edge of the table, and with one wide sweep of his arm cleared away the dishes behind her. He pressed her down onto the table and moved intimately between her thighs, allowing her the sweet sensation of having his length lodged firmly against her feminine heat. She pulled him closer, urging him on…needing more. Touching him wasn't enough. She needed him inside her.

His mouth left hers and she cried out at the loss. Her next cry was one of ecstasy as those skilled lips latched on to her breast. He suckled and laved until she thought she would explode with the mounting sensations, and then he moved to her other breast.

''Please,'' she murmured. She flexed her hips, rubbing her moistened sex along his rigid shaft.

He slipped his hand between them and parted her sensitive folds, wrenching a throaty moan from her. When one long finger slipped inside, she arched against his touch, longing for more…demanding more. He positioned himself at her entrance, using his fingers to lubricate that generous male part of him, which felt as smooth as velvet and incredibly hard against her tingling flesh.

He eased inside just a fraction—with the slightest movement—and she threatened to climax then and there. She gripped his waist and would have pulled him closer, but he stopped her.

"Wait." The single syllable was practically a growl.

She had to swallow back a scream of protest. What did he mean, *wait?* She tightened her legs around him, urging him closer. He groaned, his eyes closing with his own need. His reaction made her feel powerful. She wanted to torture him like this forever. Her inner muscles clutched greedily.

She wanted him....

But he resisted. "We need protection," he said huskily, his breath ragged.

He drew away before she could stop him, leaving her panting and on the absolute edge of orgasm. He bent down and dug around in his trousers pockets. She reached for him as the rip of foil sent anticipation searing through her all over again. She watched as he slid the condom onto his thick-ended sex, and felt the first contractions of release at the mere sight of him touching himself.

"Now." He moved back between her welcoming thighs and locked her trembling legs firmly around his waist. "Where were we?" That amber gaze burned into hers as he flattened one hand on the tabletop behind her and used the other to guide himself to the spot that throbbed insistently for him.

His eyes never leaving hers, he pushed fully into her, stretching, filling and sending her completely over the edge. They cried out together, her with release, him with the pleasure of being buried deeply inside her tight, pulsing body. It had been so very long and she had so little experience that it was almost like the first time, Shana thought, only way better.

He waited, perfectly still while she relished wave after wave of utter bliss. When she could focus once more, she saw what it cost him to hold back. Sweat had beaded on his forehead and his muscles were taut with restraint. She undulated her hips, teasing, drawing him more deeply into her heat.

Her movements shattered his control and he thrust hard and deep, again and again, his hands braced flat on the table on either side of her. She wanted to touch him all over, but she couldn't focus on anything but his face, watching the play of emotions dance there as he moved her closer and closer to that elusive pinnacle once more. Never in her life had she felt such perfect and amazing sensations. Her entire body was on fire for him alone. Nothing would ever feel as right as this—of that she was certain. And then she soared that glorious free fall once more. Sensations flooded her as her body shuddered with the delight of a second orgasm.

With a final stroke, he reached his own climax, releasing a satisfied and savage roar.

He moved slowly for a few moments longer, milking the final waves of completion from her as well as from himself, reveling in the haze of sweet, sweet pleasure.

Whatever happened from this moment forward, Shana was sure of one thing—this was what making love was supposed to be like. This wild, uncontainable desperation. Her gaze sought his and she saw the same conclusion reflected there.

This was right.

CHAPTER THIRTEEN

THEY'D MADE LOVE once more during the night. Then they'd fallen asleep in each other's arms.

Keith lay still and quiet now as dawn filled the sky. He could stay like this forever and simply watch Shana sleep. She was so very beautiful. Selfishly he wanted to touch her, but she had earned this sleep. He thought of their second round of lovemaking and his body hardened instantly. They had managed to make it upstairs and to the bed in the guest room that time. Though he'd been tempted to take her on the stairs, he'd restrained the urge, knowing full well that a little finesse was in order.

The second time had been even better than the first.

He'd thought that impossible…had been certain nothing would ever match the fervor they'd shared on the dining table. Remembered heat shivered through him. She'd been as tight as a virgin and as soft and sweet as an angel. But she'd come alive with fire in his arms. Whatever she lacked in experience, she more than made up for with plain old instinct and natural sensuality.

No woman had ever reduced him to that level of vulnerability, or tugged on his emotions, as Shana did. He could spend the rest of his life with her and never want for more. He wondered if this was the way Jaron had felt when he and Annabelle had succumbed. The pull had to be powerful for Jaron to leave behind the past.

Keith had a strong hunch that his and his friend's bachelor days might very well be over. He sighed, not with regret, but with a sort of satisfaction. No way would he have suspected that commitment felt like this. His gaze swept over her soft, sexy curves. In a few short days of forced proximity and a single night of lovemaking, she'd ruined him for anyone else.

He propped his head on his elbow and surveyed that heavenly body once more. That was not a bad thing at all. In fact, the way he saw it, he was a very lucky man. He'd found a woman who not only drove him wild sexually but challenged him intellectually, as well. Shana would definitely keep him on his toes. It was hard to believe that he'd ever considered her a mere freeloader, living off the kindness of others.

Those long-lashed lids slowly drifted open and he smiled as her eyes widened with the memories flooding back.

"Oh, my," she murmured sleepily. "I guess we really did it."

He traced the line of her cheek with one fingertip. "That we did."

Her breath caught. "The baby."

"Don't worry. I took care of her morning feeding. I wanted to let you sleep."

She smiled then. "Thanks. I definitely needed the

rest.'' She snuggled closer to him. ''I suppose we have to get in gear if we're going to make it to work this morning.''

''In a minute.'' He pressed a tender kiss to the tip of her nose. ''I want you to understand my position here.''

Trepidation filled those wide, expressive eyes. ''Keith, you don't have to make me any promises.''

''Oh, but you're wrong, Ms. Devlin.'' A grin tugged at the corners of his mouth. ''You've compromised my reputation. I'll have to hold you accountable.''

She giggled. It was the first time he'd heard her do that. He loved the sound of it. So light, so carefree…so happy.

''Well, I suppose that's true.'' She trailed one fingertip down the center of his chest and wriggled even closer. ''We'll just have to make a concerted effort at the relationship thing or risk the consequences.''

His full arousal nudged at her softness. ''For now, we have a more immediate problem.''

She reached between them and stroked his length, sending a delicious shudder through him. ''I can see that.''

Anticipation roared through him, then he stilled. Damn, he didn't have any more condoms. There'd been two in his wallet, but no more. He never brought women here…not until Shana.

''I'm afraid we're out of condoms,'' he said flatly, disappointment weighting his tone. ''I don't keep any here.''

She stroked him again, making him groan. "Oh yeah, that's right. I'm the first lover you've brought here."

He stilled her wicked hand. "Shana, you're not just a lover," he protested. "This is about a lot more than sex."

The smile that trembled across her lips pulled at his heartstrings—the heartstrings he'd only just recently realized he had.

"Are you sure about this, Keith?" She searched his eyes, hers desperate for confirmation of his words. "We're moving awfully fast here."

He cupped her face and allowed her to see in his eyes what he felt deep inside. "I'm very sure. I want to make this work. I want…you."

"Well," she said teasingly, "in that case, I think we have cause for a little celebration before we go back to the real world." Those cool little fingers escaped his hold and encircled him once more.

"Shana," he groaned. "We don't have any protection."

She waggled her brows wickedly. "Oh, but there are other things we can do, darling, that don't require that kind of protection."

Before her words fully penetrated the lust clouding his brain, she'd dived under the covers. The moment those lush lips closed around him, all thought ceased. He slumped back on the tangled sheets and let her have her way with him.

The one thought that managed to surface above the incredible ecstasy was that he would have his turn.

And she would pay dearly for every moment of sensuous torture he endured.

"YOU'RE SURE THIS IS WHAT you want to do?" Shana had to be certain.

Keith glanced at her, taking his eyes off the asphalt for a fraction of a second. "I'm positive."

She nodded and smiled. As soon as he'd redirected his attention back to the road leading to Seattle, she released a quiet breath of pure relief.

She'd promised herself she wouldn't allow these seeds of doubt to sprout, but she had trust issues, after all. Whether she wanted to admit it or not, she was scared to death that this wondrous feeling wouldn't last. That Keith would suddenly tell her it had all been a mistake.

Peeking over her shoulder at the baby, who slept peacefully in her safety carrier in the back seat, Shana vowed not to second-guess where this was going. She and Keith had made a promise to each other…a commitment.

They'd also made a commitment to the baby. Little Chris had brought them together. They wanted to keep her safe and happy until her family was found. Beyond that, they cared deeply for each other and had every intention of making this new bond work. Neither had uttered the *L* word just yet, and they certainly hadn't discussed marriage, but both were thinking along those lines. Keith didn't have to say the words, nor did she. But she could read in his every touch, his every look how much she meant to him. She hoped he could do the same with her.

God, this was so hard. No wonder they'd both avoided commitment. It was real work, not to mention frightening, dancing out on the very tip of an emotional limb without a safety net.

She turned her attention to Keith's profile. But he was worth every second of it. In her heart she knew he felt the same way.

Half an hour later as they entered Seattle proper, Shana couldn't help thinking how wrong she'd been about him when this journey had begun. She wondered if they would ever have gotten to know each other this way if the baby hadn't come into their lives. Sadness filled her when she considered that it had taken such a tragedy to make them see what was right in front of them all along.

As if picking up on her somber mood, Keith glanced at her again, careful not to linger, since morning rush hour traffic was in full spate. "You're not having second thoughts, are you?" He shrugged one shoulder. "I mean, if you are, I'd understand. This is a big step." He tightened his grip on the steering wheel. "We'll do this any way you choose. I want it to feel right to you."

She leaned over and kissed his cheek, earning herself one of those charming smiles that Keith Hewitt was famous for. "I'm okay with this. It's the right thing for us and for the baby."

He reached for her hand and grasped it firmly in his own. "We'll have a few bumps on the way, but anything worth having is worth working for.'' When he stopped for a traffic light, he turned to her, his amber gaze steady and sincere. ''My father always said that.''

Tears welled in her eyes and she had to fight to hold them back. ''Your father was a very smart man.'' She took the opportunity to silently thank God for the wonderful father Keith had been blessed with. He had turned his young son into such a fine man.

Leaving that tender subject for now, they traveled the rest of the way to the hospital in silence, their fingers entwined as a sign of their commitment to each other.

She'd been right when she'd told Brett about Keith. He was the one. She was certain of it. He would never let her down. Nor she him. This was just the beginning. She couldn't say whether marriage and children were in their future together, but she could say love was there. She could feel it all around them. She prayed Baby Chris could feel it, as well. For however long it took to find the infant's real parents or any surviving family, Shana wanted Chris to feel the love of those around her.

Keith held the door for Shana as they entered the hospital's spacious lobby. He couldn't help the expression of pride on his face. She was his in every sense of the word, and he wanted the world to know it.

They greeted friends and co-workers as they made their way toward Round the Clock, and it would have been impossible to miss the whispers and startled gazes that followed their path. He had a reputation, and everyone likely knew by now that he and Shana had spent the weekend together. With the baby, of course, but that part would be left out of the equation. The gossip would be about him and Shana alone.

But he didn't care. Everyone would soon see that this time was different.

While they waited for the elevator to arrive, he bent down and kissed Shana's cheek, giving their audience something to really talk about. And if things went the way he hoped, he'd soon give them something else— more tangible evidence—to add to the rumor mill.

Outside Round the Clock, Keith set the baby's diaper bag near the door and gave Shana a lingering kiss goodbye. He had to get to his office and he wasn't about to get caught up in the interrogation Alexandra would no doubt start the moment she saw them together. Alexandra Webber was, after all, Shana's sister. She would demand to know what was going on and maybe even what Keith's intentions were. Right now, he planned to keep those to himself. He wanted just the right moment with Shana…alone.

SHANA FELT THE SMILE on her face as she watched Keith board the elevator, headed for his own office. Before the doors closed, he waved and then shot her a wink, which sent a little shiver all the way to her bones. God, how she loved that man.

It was true. She was *in* love. Though the realization scared her just a little, it felt good. She missed Keith already.

Before she had time to dwell on his absence, Alex rushed to open the door leading into the center. "Shana, you're back!" She ushered Shana and the baby into the child-friendly lobby and hugged them both. After a moment of fussing over the little one, Alexandra smiled at her stepsister. "It's so good to see you." Then she immediately adopted a stern expression and demanded, "Why didn't you call me? I didn't hear until this morning that you'd changed shifts."

Shana blushed, embarrassed at the oversight. It had been a while since she'd had someone who worried about her. Not that her brother didn't worry, but he sure never let it show. "I'm sorry, Alex. I just got busy and…"

Wearing an odd expression, Alex studied Shana, first her face, especially her eyes, and then a full up and down sweep. "What's going on, Shana?" she asked, just a hint of suspicion in her tone. "What's happened between you and our hospital Romeo?"

Shana chewed her lower lip to buy time, but Alex narrowed her gaze, silently warning that she wouldn't wait long. "Well, it's kind of complicated."

A broad grin spread over her stepsister's face. "I knew you two had a thing for each other! I knew it! Any fool could see the sparks flying."

Thankfully, a dozen or so toddlers and preschoolers flooded into the lobby just then in search of their caregiver, saving Shana from having to explain in detail.

How could Alex have known when Shana hadn't? Shaking off the troubling thought, she greeted the children she'd missed so much. They hugged her legs and begged to see Baby Chris. Just this once, she and Alex allowed the kids to gather in the lobby, which was normally against the rules. The children were excited to see Shana and curious about the new baby.

All but Todd Jamison, of course. He was busy running around the group like a wild man. The child could not be still even for a minute. But deep down he was a sweetheart. Shana simply shook her head and let the boy be a boy.

The next thing she knew, a couple of nurses arrived to drop off their children, and quickly surrounded Shana. One had brought along her cousin, a new member of staff, to see what a wonderful child-care center the hospital was so fortunate to have. They had all heard about the mystery baby and wanted to see her.

"So this is what all the ruckus is about," observed Clara Thompson, a nurse from the pediatric ward. The lobby was so crowded she could scarcely take a step inside.

"She's just adorable," Alex murmured, a dreamy smile on her face as she gazed down at the baby. Alex wanted children of her own, that was easy to see.

Shana hoped her stepsister's upcoming marriage to Ben would bring her all that she dreamed of. Alex deserved that and more. She was so loving and she'd suffered so much in her life.

Kind of like herself, Shana reasoned. Although she'd had a pretty good life as a child, there had been things she'd missed out on, like a steady father and a confident mother. Every instinct assured her that Keith was going to make up for that. She smiled down at the baby. And maybe one day soon they would have a baby of their own.

Shana's smile faded. But what would become of this tiny infant? Where were her parents? Were they alive? Did they want her? Shana's heart ached at the possibilities. No, she told herself, little Chris was going to be fine. She and Keith would see to that.

"Todd!"

Shana's head came up at Alex's cry of distress.

"Someone stop him! He's on the elevator!"

It took a few seconds for Shana to realize what was happening. Todd had escaped past Clara and slipped into one of the elevators. Dear Lord, if he got loose in the hospital...

Alex, followed by two other women, rushed to the elevator, but it was too late. Shana watched from the child-care center entranceway, her hands full with the baby and the children, who were now crowded around the glass door. The elevator started its descent, the numbers lighting up one after the other.

Shana rushed to the desk and grabbed the telephone there. She quickly entered the number for security. The seconds it took to alert them felt like hours, but their reaction was swift and decisive. Just when Alex would have darted into the stairwell to rush after him, Shana called out to her. "They've got him two floors down. One of the nurses is holding him until security gets there."

The crowd in the lobby heaved a collective sigh of

relief. Thank God. A child missing, even for a few short minutes, was the nightmare all parents and child care providers feared the most.

Mere minutes later, Todd, accompanied by a security guard who looked like a linebacker on a professional football team, waltzed back into the center. The child clearly had not a repentant bone in his body.

Alex immediately took custody of the rascal and gave him a stern talking to. Shana resettled the children after the excitement of seeing the armed guard. They'd certainly started this morning out with a bang.

As she moved among the children, overseeing their finger painting, her mind drifted back to Keith. Baby Chris was sleeping in the nursery, safe and sound for the time being. Keith was no doubt checking in with Jaron and Seth to find out if there was any news where the baby was concerned. Word that the man and woman who'd died in the car crash weren't the biological parents of the infant would soon hit the media, if it hadn't already.

Shana was a whole weekend behind in the news. One of the mothers had told her about a child stalker that had everyone scared to death. She remembered the headlines from a couple of weeks ago, but had hoped that whoever was behind the gruesome crimes had been stopped by now. She shivered. If Todd had managed to flee the building, he would have been vulnerable to that sort of crime.

How could anyone harm a child? Shana couldn't

fathom the kind of twisted mind it took to do such a thing.

"Shana."

She looked up to find Alex surveying the room, her face ashen with worry.

"What's wrong?" Shana's heart kicked into a faster rhythm. What on earth had happened now?

"Count heads for me, would you? I'm coming up with fourteen instead of fifteen, and I've checked every nook and cranny around here."

A renewed rush of adrenaline made Shana's scalp tingle. She quickly counted the children, adding little Chris to the lot. "Fourteen," she said distractedly, doing a mental rundown of the names.

"God," Alex breathed. "Someone's missing."

Todd was here, so it wasn't him.

Who, then?

Both Alex and Shana surveyed the children. Shana repeated the names in her head as she verified each angelic little face. Ricky Dorsey...

"Tina."

Dear God. Jaron's daughter.

"I'll call security!" Alex snatched up the cordless handset lying on a nearby table.

"I'll check the corridors." Shana rushed through the maze of children and into the lobby. Outside the main door, the corridor was empty. The elevators sat eerily still.

She flew to the stairwell door and pushed it open. "Tina! Tina!" No answer. No sound of footfalls on the treads.

The headlines everyone had been talking about during the time Todd was missing flashed in her mind.

How had this happened?

She hurried back into the center to find Alex just ending a call.

"She's gone," Shana said in a rush. "How could this have happened twice in one morning?"

"It had to be when we were trying to stop Todd. Security is scouring the hospital." Alex placed her hand over her mouth and visibly tried to calm herself. "We have to find her," she whispered, the words scarcely audible. "We have to."

Shana drew Alex into her arms. "We will." She hugged her sister tightly and prayed that God would keep the little girl safe until someone located her. God, she was only four years old.

Alex drew back. "But what if we don't?"

The stark fear in her eyes matched the horror twisting in Shana's chest. "We will. We have to."

"If she manages to leave the building—"

"She won't," Shana insisted. "Do you hear me, Alex? She won't. She's going to be fine."

A little hand tugged at Shana's slacks. She peered down to find five-year-old Ricky Dorsey staring up at her. "It's okay, sweetie," she tried to assure him, but her voice wobbled just the tiniest bit. "Sit down with the other boys and girls and we'll have storytime a little early today."

His small face scrunched up in worry. "But, Shana, where's my sister?"

His words echoed all the way to Shana's soul. If only she knew...

CHAPTER FOURTEEN

KEITH FOUND SHANA in the nursery, tending Baby Chris. For a moment he had to stand back and simply watch. The vision of woman and child very nearly took his breath away. His mind immediately conjured the image of her holding his child…their child. For the first time in his life he really wanted that. He knew there would be doubts from time to time, insecurities from the loss of his mother and all he'd suffered as a child, but he was strong enough to conquer them. With Shana by his side, he could do most anything.

He'd gotten back to his office this morning only to be faced with yet another life-altering decision. He'd received a completely unexpected call offering him a district-wide position as Child Services director for the state. The position offered the opportunity to help children on a much larger scale, and the salary was outstanding. There was no denying that he was flattered, but he'd declined without hesitation. He wasn't about to ask Shana to pull up roots and move away with him when she'd only just gotten to know her new family. He'd made a promise to Shana and to Baby Chris. He wasn't going back on those promises. In fact, he wasn't going to mention the offer and risk making her feel guilty about his decision. It was his choice. It was made; end of story.

Once she'd settled the baby into a crib, he approached her. Hearing his footsteps, she turned to greet whoever had entered the room, and the agony on her face constricted his chest.

Hope flared in her eyes. "Is there any news?"

He hated to disappoint her. "No. Sorry." Tina Dorsey was still missing.

Shana's expression crumpled. "Why can't they find her?"

Unable to bear seeing her like this, he drew her into his arms and held her tightly to his heart. "They'll find her. She's here somewhere."

"But what if she's not?" Shana murmured. "You should have seen Jaron… Oh, God, it was so awful. And Annabelle. She was almost as devastated as he was."

Keith caressed her back soothingly. "The entire Seattle police force is here, I think." He eased her slightly away from him and fixed a steady gaze on her watery one. "They've widened the search perimeter for more than a mile around the hospital. She couldn't have gotten farther than that on her own. They'll find her."

Her chin trembled. "But what if she isn't on her own? What if—"

He shook his head, cutting off her words. "No. We're not going to think like that. My guess is she's still in the hospital. She may have crawled under some gurney somewhere and fallen asleep." His fingers tightened reassuringly around Shana's arms. "She's here. I know it."

If only Shana could have that much faith. She'd managed to try to reassure Alex, but beneath the brave front she'd adopted, she was terrified. She sank against Keith's chest and thanked God for his presence. She'd been ready to shatter into a thousand screaming pieces of agony. Alex was walking around the center in a near state of shock. Shana couldn't get her to settle down. Even Ben hadn't been able to calm her completely, but his presence had been immensely helpful.

The afternoon shift had arrived at the center early to help out during the crisis, though all the children except little Chris had been transported to Forrester Square Day Care for the rest of the day. It was important that the other children have a calm environment. Although two people were required to man the phones, which rang continuously, still there was no news. Shana said another quick prayer for the little girl's safety.

"How do people do it?" she murmured, more to herself than to Keith.

He pressed a tender kiss to her forehead. "What do you mean?"

She shook her head and allowed the images to replay in her mind. She'd thought of nothing else for hours. "I can't stop thinking about the horror on Jaron's face…the anguish on Annabelle's." She pulled away a little so she could look into Keith's eyes. "How can a person bring a child into this world, knowing all the things that can go wrong? The birth defects, the accident possibilities, the dangers. It has to be as scary as hell from the moment a child is born. What if you make a mistake? Forget something you shouldn't? The slightest misstep could end in tragedy.''

Keith pulled her back into his arms and held her tightly. ''You can only hope for the best,'' he told her softly. ''We can't stop living life because we fear death.''

He grew strangely still, and Shana knew in an instant what he was thinking. He was remembering his mother, and how that loss had affected his ability to make a commitment.

Shana lifted her gaze to his once more. ''You okay?''

He shook his head and laughed, but the sound held no humor. ''I was just thinking that that's exactly what I've been doing all this time. I've allowed the fear of death—of any kind of loss—to keep me from enjoying the life I've been blessed with.''

She had to kiss him…to drive those shadows from his handsome face. The kiss was urgent, with both of them needing the physical connection, the comfort of the tenuous bond they'd formed.

''Shana!''

She and Keith jumped apart at the sound of Alex's strained voice. Tears were flowing down her cheeks but she was smiling…smiling through her tears.

''They found her! She's safe. Tina is safe.''

Keith, Shana and Alex rushed up to Annabelle's

apartment, where a blessed family reunion was taking place. Carleen stayed behind with Baby Chris.

Tina, it seemed, had never left the hospital. She'd remembered visiting Annabelle's place and had wanted to go there again—to make hats, of all things. She'd recalled the floor number and apartment number, as well as where Annabelle kept her spare key. Shana had known the child was bright, but hadn't suspected she was so fearless. She shook her head, weary and relieved. Thank God the little girl had never been in any real danger. Thank God!

Shana and Keith got to witness Jaron and his children's proposal to Annabelle. Tina and Ricky invited her to become their new mom. It was so moving. Every woman present cried, and even some of the men looked a little bleary-eyed. It was the most beautiful proposal Shana could imagine, and no one was more deserving to be Tina and Ricky's new mom than her dear friend Annabelle.

"I should clear things up in my office so we can get out of here for the day," Keith finally said, his lips very near her ear to ensure that she heard him over the hoopla going on around them.

She nodded, and with a quick peck on her cheek, he disappeared. She supposed she should do the same. Take care of a few final details at the center, first and foremost her work schedule for the next few weeks, and then make her way with the baby up to Keith's office to go home.

Home. Her heart welled at the idea as she headed for the elevator. Just a hint of panic niggled at her as

she realized how easily she'd come to think of Keith
and his cabin as home. But it was true, she did feel
at home there. Maybe she could tempt her brother into
coming to Seattle by telling him all about the cabin
and the nearby creek.

"Wasn't that just the sweetest thing? And such a
relief that the little girl was safe. We'd all feared the
worse, what with those awful headlines lately."

Shana produced a thankful smile for the woman
who'd spoken. Two nurses and a secretary had
walked into the elevator with her. "It really is a bless-
ing," she agreed.

One of the nurses looked around, as if making sure
it was all right to speak freely. Then she said, "Can
you believe Dr. Peters is actually in love? I didn't
know the woman had a heart."

Shana bit her tongue. It was true that most of the
staff considered Annabelle somewhat of an ice queen.
"I think it's just marvelous. They both deserve good
things."

A round of nods and sounds of approval filled the
elevator in response to her statement. Well, good for
her. She'd headed off that bout of gossip.

"You have to tell us, Shana," a nurse named Kelli
urged. She waggled her brows. "How was your
weekend with Keith Hewitt?"

Shana stiffened. "We…we had a lovely time."

The other nurse, whose name Shana couldn't recall
at the moment, hee-hawed with laughter that bordered
on being rude. "Come on, girl, don't give us that."
She sent Shana a pointed look followed by an enthu-

siastic thumbs-up. "We've all heard he's a god in the sack. Is it true? Are you planning to see him again? Or is he moving on already?"

Kelli patted Shana on the arm. "Moving on is his MO, you know. Are you going to be heartbroken?" She sighed wistfully. "I know I would be. But I'll bet it was worth it."

"Well, he won't be around to pine over, anyway," the secretary said knowingly. "His secretary told me he's gotten a great job offer from the state. He'll be leaving the hospital."

Kelli grinned. "At least you managed to get yourself a taste before it was too late," she said to Shana.

Thankfully, the elevator doors opened just then. "Excuse me." Shana rushed out, barely holding back the tears before she escaped the expectant gazes of the thoughtless women.

"Honey, I didn't mean anything!" Kelli shouted after her, but the doors closed before she could say more.

Shana knew they hadn't meant to hurt her. It had all been in good fun. Keith did, after all, have a reputation. He was known for his love 'em and leave 'em attitude. She'd known that well—had despised him for it.

And now she was in love with him. He'd told her not to believe everything she heard. And she didn't. That nonsense wasn't what bothered her. Not really. It was the job offer. Why hadn't he told her? She refused to believe that he'd taken the job and simply avoided telling her. There was more to it than that. Had he turned it down? For her?

Unable to help herself she dashed into the nearest ladies' room and had herself a good cry. After watching those heartfelt moments with Annabelle and Jaron her emotions were already raw. What if he had turned the job down? What if he grew to resent her because of the missed opportunity? If he'd really wanted the job and had turned it down... She swallowed tightly. But then, what if that secretary had been right? What if he was leaving?

Shana cursed herself. Here she was crying her eyes out instead of simply asking him what actually happened. Where was her trust? She was supposed to trust the man she loved. How silly she was. With a deep reaffirming breath, Shana cooled her flushed face with damp paper towels and scrubbed away what makeup she hadn't cried off. Without her purse she had no way to repair it and that was just as well. Even the best foundation wouldn't cover up smudges that dark or the swelling her emotional bout had caused.

When she'd pulled herself together enough, she stepped out into the corridor and headed for Round the Clock. She had details to take care of and Chris to prepare for the journey to Keith's cabin.

She almost frowned when she realized she hadn't thought of his place as home this time. Shana shook herself. Was she so unsure of herself and of Keith that she'd let something as foolish as plain old gossip devastate her this way?

Apparently so.

But that wasn't fair to him. She never wanted to be accused again of allowing first impressions to rule her. From the moment she'd signed on with the hospital and gotten a glimpse of the infamous Keith Hewitt, she had allowed all she heard to color her judgment. Well, she'd also been attracted to him deep down, and hated herself for that weakness.

She owed Keith better than that. But years of distrusting good-looking men—men in general, actually—made her doubt herself even now. However, it was well past time that she stopped blaming her mother for instilling such doubt in her. It was time that Shana rose above that one flaw in her upbringing and allowed the trust that had built between her and Keith to guide her.

Whatever the future held for them, she would not ruin it by being too afraid to allow it to happen. What good was life if you didn't live it?

Not a hell of a lot.

Squaring her shoulders and putting a new determination in her step, Shana went straight to Keith's office. She had to see him, to reconfirm all that she knew in her heart.

By the time she walked into his office, she'd developed a healthy case of irritation at herself and the female staff in general. Why hadn't she said something? It was no one's fault but her own if her reaction fed the rumors. Keith deserved better than that.

Keith's secretary looked up and smiled automatically. "Hello, may I help you?"

"I'd like to see Ke—Mr. Hewitt." The request

came out a little more firmly than she'd intended. Silently she scolded herself for taking such a tone with an innocent victim. Marcelle Jackson was a nice older woman who went out of her way to be pleasant to everyone.

"Oh, I'm sorry, Ms. Devlin, he's out for the moment." Marcelle quickly flipped through his messages. "He's having coffee with a Ms. Nelson from the state office in the staff lounge. May I leave him a message?"

Shana was sure that when the secretary looked up, she would be startled to find her gone. But Shana had heard all she needed to. If he was turning down that job—or taking it—he should have discussed the decision with her first. Fury pulsed through her as she marched straight to the lounge. Well, there was no time like the present to find out.

She burst through the door and stopped midstep as her eyes took in the scene. The woman sat on the sofa to the left of Keith, who occupied an armchair. Both held disposable coffee cups and looked up to see who'd intruded so abruptly on their meeting.

"Are you taking the job?" Shana demanded.

Startled, the woman glanced up at her, then back at Keith. "I'm afraid he's declined my offer," she said with regret.

Shana immediately flushed with humiliation as she considered how this must look. How she must appear with her makeup gone, washed off by her tears, and her aggressive stance.

Keith stood immediately and held out his hand.

"Ms. Nelson, this is Shana Devlin." His smile was wide and welcoming. "Shana—" he inclined his head toward the other woman "—this is Ms. Nelson from Child Services. I was just telling her how much we enjoyed taking care of the baby this past weekend, and that I'm afraid her visit has been a waste of time. I'm happy right here in Seattle."

If lightning had struck her and put her out of her misery, Shana would have felt so much better. But it didn't, and she had no choice but to move forward, taking the hand Keith offered. What a fool she was.

"Ms. Devlin…" Ms. Nelson stood and offered her own hand, giving Shana's free one a brisk shake. "I'd like to thank you for so kindly offering your time to be there for this child. It takes a special kind of person to act so selflessly. We need more people like you and Mr. Hewitt. We've had our eye on him for some time now."

Shana managed a thank-you, and the rest of the conversation was a little lost on her. She spent the entire time kicking herself for intruding. She should have waited for Keith to talk to her. He would have…eventually. With all that had gone on that morning, he probably hadn't had time to tell her about the job offer. She thought of his visit to Round the Clock earlier and how upset she'd been. No wonder he hadn't mentioned it then.

She watched as Keith charmed Ms. Nelson, realizing as he did so the true nature of his affability. Yes, he did charm the ladies. Yes, he was a smooth talker. But it was in the best interest of those under his care. A smile stretched across Shana's lips as pride welled within her. Seattle Memorial was truly fortunate to have such a fine man on its staff.

Somehow she'd have to make up to him for this temporary lapse. She had definitely learned her lesson. Trust went far deeper than mere talk; it went all the way to the heart. Her heart.

When Ms. Nelson had gone, he turned to Shana and sighed. "I'm sorry you had to find out like this."

She looked up at him in earnest. "Please tell me you didn't make this decision solely because of me. I don't want you to regret it later."

Keith took her into his arms. "Shana, the main reason I didn't take that job was because I love my work here. But I'd be lying if I said that you didn't enter into the equation. You'll be entering into all my future decisions."

"But what if—"

"No buts," he interrupted smoothly. "I made the best decision for *our* future. My only regret is that I didn't recognize sooner how much I want you."

KEITH PAUSED in the doorway of the bedroom they'd spent the better part of the evening turning into a nursery. He watched as Shana tucked the baby into the new crib with its Winnie the Pooh bumper pads. Shana was so beautiful. He suddenly hoped that their first child was a girl...a girl who looked just like her mother.

"Is she asleep?" he whispered when Shana stood there for a while, staring down into the crib.

She looked up and smiled, then nodded. "Come see."

He slipped across the room to stand by Shana and peer into the crib. The baby slept soundly, her little lips puckered. "She's beautiful," he murmured.

Shana hugged his arm and nodded in agreement. "I just hope we find out soon where she came from."

Keith tucked her hand into his. "Come sit outside with me."

He led the way down the stairs and out onto the back stoop. When they were settled comfortably, Shana seated between his legs and leaning against his chest, he pointed to the sky. "See all those stars?"

"They're lovely. It's so beautiful up here, Keith." She turned in his arms and looked up at him. "I almost hate to move back to the city."

"We'll come back later, when things are settled."

Shana knew he was talking about the baby. "She's so precious. The police have to find her family. Can you imagine if her parents are alive, how they must feel with her lost to them?"

A moment of silence followed as they both remembered the reunion between Jaron and his little girl. "No parent should have to go through that horror. There just has to be a happy ending."

Keith hugged Shana closer to him, and she could feel his heart beat reassuringly against her back.

"They're searching near the border right now," he told her. "Somewhere they'll find her parents. Just think how glad they'll be that we've taken such good care of her for them."

That much was true. Shana knew with certainty that she would want someone like Keith to take care of her child if it was missing—if she had a child. The mere idea squeezed her heart. "I'm praying night and day for that happy ending," she said firmly. "Jaron and Annabelle have their family now...they got a happy ending. Chris has to have one, too. I won't believe anything else."

"Neither will I," Keith agreed solemnly.

Shana and Keith sat on the back steps of the cabin for a long time that night, staring up at the stars, wrapped in the joy and warmth of the love growing between them. It was all so very perfect. The day had been a wild one, what with Todd's little exploit, Tina's disappearance and the unexpected job offer. It had been nearly too much to bear. But watching Jaron and Annabelle publicly proclaim their love for each other had been the ultimate happy ending.

In spite of all there was to be thankful for, Shana found her thoughts going back to the mystery baby. "Do you think Chris's parents are looking for her at this very moment?"

Keith shrugged. "I don't know. Seems as if there would be an APB if anyone had reported a missing child. But the authorities are doing all they can with what they have. Somehow they'll find them. It'll just take time."

Shana thought about the conversation she'd had with Annabelle yesterday. "Why do you think the woman kept insisting that Annabelle tell no one?"

The night sounds were the only response for a time,

then Keith finally admitted, "I don't know. Maybe we never will. But on a night like this, anything is possible. It's a night of miracles." He shrugged again. "Look up at that sky, Shana, and tell me that there are any real secrets at all."

Tell no one...

"Someone knows," he murmured softly. "Somewhere, someone knows."

Shana shifted in his arms, turning to drape hers around his neck. "There's something I know, Mr. Hewitt."

Those long-fingered hands molded to her back, emanating strength and an affection that almost took her breath. "What is it you know, Ms. Devlin?" he asked silkily.

"That I trust you and I'm pretty sure I'm in love with you."

The smile he gifted her with very nearly undid her completely. "Oh, I hope so, Ms. Devlin, because I'd sure hate to be in this boat all alone."

He backed up those words with the sweetest kiss, and Shana knew that faith, having gotten them this far, would take them all the way. Just as it would take the mystery baby where she needed to be.

HARLEQUIN®
Makes any time special ®

HARLEQUIN®
AMERICAN *Romance*

Upbeat, All-American Romances

HARLEQUIN®
Duets™

Romantic Comedy

Harlequin® Historical

Historical, Romantic Adventure

HARLEQUIN®
INTRIGUE

Romantic Suspense

Harlequin Romance®

Capturing the World You Dream Of

HARLEQUIN® *Presents*

Seduction and passion guaranteed

HARLEQUIN® *Super* **ROMANCE**®

Emotional, Exciting, Unexpected

HARLEQUIN®
Temptation

Sassy, Sexy, Seductive!

HDIR1